AF489940

A Mississippi Summer

JASON A. BEVERLY

A MISSISSIPPI SUMMER

Copyright © 2022 by Jason A. Beverly. All rights reserved, including the right to reproduce this book or any portion thereof, in any form. No part of this publication may be reproduced, distributed, or transmitted in any form or by any means, including photocopying, recording, or other electronic or mechanical methods, without the prior written permission of the publisher, except in the case of brief quotations embodied in critical reviews and certain other noncommercial uses permitted by copyright law.

ISBN: 9798836210458

DEDICATION

I dedicate this book to my family, friends, fans, and everyone else seeking a summer escape. Thanks to my wonderful wife, Monique, for supporting my literary endeavors and ensuring they remain entertaining and logical. I thank my son, Mason, for keeping my work relevant and contemporary. To my daughter Morgan, I am grateful for you helping me create characters and storylines. I thank my mom, Deffene, for being my hero and inspiring me to be the best I can be. I thank my sisters LaKenya and Samantha for always supporting and promoting my work.

A MISSISSIPPI SUMMER

A MISSISSIPPI SUMMER

CONTENTS

vi

A MISSISSIPPI SUMMER

INTRODUCTION

A lovely crescent moon falls over the dark silhouette of a house, the only livable structure within a two-mile radius. The street lamp along the road in front of the property flickers, periodically scaring away the moths, mayflies, and beetles that have gathered. The cicadas' choruses resound across the vast, green fields around the home, not to be equaled by the crickets' chirping stridulating.

A faint glow emanates from within the house's opened side window. And a dripping sound also echoes from there.

***

Inside, the television emits the only hint of light. An opened pizza box, revealing four slices, rests on the coffee table. Jude Triton Desonier, an attractive young guy with natural, wavy hair and a scruffy five-o'clock shadow, leans back on the couch. He appears on the verge of falling asleep with the remote in his hand. And despite the dripping noise from the kitchen growing louder and louder, he shuts his eyes and succumbs to sleep.

***

Circa the summer of 1980, several people in vintage swim attire fill a Pensacola beach, where chatter and laughter echo abound. While some folks play volleyball and football, others sunbathe and read their favorite books. Amid the bustling activity, a young boy sits on a colorful towel, building a sandcastle. The red paper sailor hat he wears perfectly matches his crimson swim trunks.

Suddenly, a gust of wind comes through, knocking the hat off the child's head and carrying it towards the sea. And the boy stands up and chases after it, oblivious to those around.

But soon, a female voice shouts, "Jude, no!"

And the child stops running. He glances around but doesn't notice anyone familiar.

So he turns and heads towards the sea again. But before he can get to the water, a feminine hand grabs his pudgy right arm. And when he turns around and looks up, the sun's glare nearly blinds him, forcing him to close his eyes.

***

Back in the present, a late-night talk show plays on the television, still projecting the only light in the dark living room. Jude remains asleep on the couch. But a short time later, he blinks his eyes open. After he sits up, he sighs and shakes his head.

"Stupid dream," he mumbles, his voice thick with a southern Louisiana accent.

But he knows the memory he recalled was the truth confronted on his third birthday when he discovered his pleasure at the beach would never extend beyond the sand.

"What a life," he says, closing the pizza box and grabbing it.

He stands up and walks towards the kitchen.

***

Inside the kitchen, darkness reigns, and nothing is visible.

But then there's a flash of light from the refrigerator opening. And as Jude places the pizza box inside, a mouse runs across his feet and scurries behind the stove.

"I'll get you eventually," he mumbles, closing the fridge and restoring total blackness.

And his footsteps reverberate as he walks toward the living room in the dark.

***

Inside the dusky living room, an infomercial plays on the television, still emitting the space's only illumination. Jude sits on the couch and leans back. He looks at the TV with heavy eyes, bobbing his head and nodding off now and again. He finally falls asleep a little while later.

CHAPTER 1

The following morning, a faded-blue pickup truck with Terrebonne Parish license plates rests in the overgrown front yard of a modest, fair-condition, dingy white house. A barking dog echoes in the distance as a late-90s black sports car zooms by on the dirty road, leaving an orange, dusty cloud in its wake.

The weatherman's voice echoes from the television inside through the open side window, stating, "Folks, today will be another hot one in south Louisiana, where temps can surpass one hundred degrees."

***

Modern-but-inexpensive furniture and decor fill the interior of the living room where Jude is asleep on the couch. Suddenly, he opens his eyes and stares at the weatherman on TV. Sweat seeps from his skin's pores despite the ceiling fan spinning above him and the white box fan on the floor blowing straight at him.

As Jude stares at the television, he becomes sleepy again, his piercing gray eyes occasionally shutting and his head jerking. But he soon becomes alert, yawning loudly and stretching.

"Ugh," he grumbles a short time later. "The yard."

A loud vehicle horn suddenly echoes from outside, prompting Jude to cringe.

"What the heck!" he shouts, leaping to his feet and sprinting to the open window.

He peers outside of it to see the rear of his best friend Colton "Colt" LeDuff's red, mid-70s muscle car speeding up the road, leaving a trail of orange dust in the air behind it.

"Colt," he mumbles, shaking his head and smiling.

He sighs, turns, and heads toward the kitchen. As he walks across the rickety floors, they creak loudly. But after six years of renting the old house, none of its unique oddities and sounds bother him anymore.

***

It's quiet inside the tiny kitchen, filled with low-end appliances and lighting fixtures. Suddenly, Jude enters it and glances at the clock on the microwave, which displays a time of 8:14.

"Darned," he says, frowning and making his way to the fridge. "It's only morning-time, but it's burning up. I need to hurry and hit the yard before it gets hotter."

He opens the refrigerator and peers inside at the milk, eggs, cheese, bottled waters, a box of pizza, and soon-to-expire cold cuts. And shortly after, he scratches his head, frowning as if disappointed.

"Looks like it'll be an egg sandwich again," he remarks, sighing.

But before he can grab the carton of eggs, the black landline phone on the counter rings. So he closes the fridge and picks up the phone. He glances at the caller ID and sees that his father, Joachim Desonier, is calling. So he answers it.

"Hey, Pops," he greets him. "What's up?"

"Oh, nothing much," Joachim replies, his accent and speech sounding similar to Jude's. "Just checking to see if you were up."

"I'm up," Jude responds. "Why?"

"Well, I ran into Hilliard at the bank the other day," Joachim explains. "He told me you ain't been keeping that yard up."

"Seriously?" Jude asks, rolling his eyes. "What goes on over here is none of his business."

"But that's his house, son," Joachim points out.

"Yeah, but I pay him rent," Jude states emphatically. "And I ain't been late with a payment since I've been here."

"And I applaud you for that," Joachim tells him. "But you are living on someone else's property, son. Yeah, you pay rent. But part of that agreement also calls for you to maintain the grounds. Come on, Jude! You know this."

Frustrated, Jude stares at the ceiling and shakes his head. Soon after, he takes a deep breath and exhales it.

"Look, Pops, I get it," he tells Joachim. "I know you and Mr. Lafitte go way back, and I ain't trying to mess that up. And I appreciate you for talking him into renting this place to me. So, I'm going to do better for both of y'all. I'm about to go do the yard now."

"Good!" Joachim states. "That's the Desonier spirit!"

"Right," Jude says, grinning. "Anyway, I'll talk to you later, Pops."

"Okay, but one more thing before you go," Joachim replies.

"Yes, sir. What is it?"

"How are your finances, son?"

"Why?"

"Because we still receive some of your mail here at the house. And you got a lot of overdue bills."

"I know, but you and Momma ain't got to worry about that. I'll take care of it."

"But you owe some of everybody. You're still at the plant, right?"

"Yes, sir. But it's not like it used to be. They've been cutting our hours, and some folks heard they're thinking about shutting down the plant."

"Oh, I see. Do we need to loan you a little something until you get back on your feet?"

"Nah, I'm good, Pops. I got some things lined up."

"Like what?"

"For starters, a potential job in Mississippi."

"Doing what?"

"Construction, in Gulfport. If I get the job, I'll be part of a crew rebuilding a casino destroyed by

Hurricane Katrina. It'll only be for the summer, but the pay will be great."

"Well, hopefully, it'll work out. And if it does, stay out of that water. It's dangerous."

"Yeah, yeah, yeah. Seawater will give me lesions on my legs."

"Certain nutrients in the water cause the pain and lesions. Just be careful, son. You could end up in the hospital."

"So I've heard, most of my life. It's why I never learned how to swim."

"Look, son, I'm sorry. But it's hereditary."

"I know, which is why you shouldn't apologize. Besides, I got it from Momma, remember?"

"How could I not remember?"

"Anyway, you have my word, Pops. If I get the job, I won't go in the water. Well, um, I got to go. But I'll keep you posted on everything."

"Um, wait, son!"

"What is it, Pops?"

"Um, you ever think about moving back to Houma? They got plenty of high-paying jobs here."

"Nah. I know you and Momma love it there, but I don't care for it."

"But it's your hometown."

"And that's the reason I don't want to be there. I don't constantly want to run into folks I graduated high school with, only for them to deem me a failure because I don't have a fancy job or university degree. But they'll probably be correct. I mean, my current situation doesn't exactly shout success."

"Don't be so hard on yourself, Jude. You once owned a small, profitable construction company and fell on hard times. That's all. You'll bounce back."

"Yeah, I hope so."

"But anyway, I understand why you feel that way about Houma," Joachim says to Jude. "But what about Bayou Cane? Plenty of jobs there as well."

"I'm good, Pops," Jude tells him. "Other than working at the plant, construction work is what I do best. I got faith the gig in Gulfport will pan out and help me relaunch my construction business."

"Perhaps," Joachim replies.

"Anyway, I got to go," Jude says to him. "Tell Momma hi for me."

CHAPTER 2

Later, a sweaty Jude rests in a chair on the front porch, sipping a bottle of cold water and admiring the yardwork he did. He feels good about himself, so he smiles. And he belches loudly soon after.

"Oops," he says, embarrassed, covering his mouth and glancing around. "My bad."

And as he continues to gaze around, he notices a blue, American-made luxury car pull up in front of the house and stop. Its tinted driver's side window drops, revealing Hilliard Lafitte, an older, bald-headed man.

"Hey!" he calls out to Jude in a raspy Cajun accent.

"How about it, Mr. Lafitte?" Jude responds, waving.

Hilliard waves and glances around the yard, appearing satisfied. He then looks at Jude.

"You talked to your daddy, huh?" he asks him.

"Sir?" Jude calls out with a shrug, confused.

Hilliard points to the grass and says, "The yard."

"Oh," Jude says. "Yes, sir. We talked this morning. I told him I would do a better job maintaining the yard."

"Well, it looks good," Hilliard points out, nodding.

"Appreciate that, Mr. Lafitte," Jude responds with a smile and nod. "So, what brings you around these parts today?"

"Just checking up on my property around the corner," Hilliard answers.

"Talking about the purple house on Bovine?" Jude asks.

"Yep, that one," Hilliard confirms. "Anyway, I was heading back to Schriever when the yard caught my attention. It's been a while since I've seen it look this nice. Anyway, I stopped when I saw you on that there porch. And, um, I'm glad I did. I want to talk to you about something."

"Oh, okay," Jude says, nervously swallowing. "Um, what is it?"

"Give me a minute," Hilliard tells him, turning the car off, opening the door, and getting out.

After he closes the door, he heads towards the porch, limping. Jude keeps a straight face despite the shock of noticing the man's sickly-looking appearance, behavior, and demeanor.

And when Hilliard finally makes it to the porch and sits in a chair, he finds Jude avoiding eye contact with him.

"It's okay, son," he tells Jude. "I know that I look a mess."

"You lost a little weight, but so what?" Jude says. "I

can stand to lose a few pounds."

Hilliard smirks and remarks, "I appreciate what you did there, but no need to get all soft on me. Instead, try asking me if something is wrong."

Jude nods, clears his throat, and says, "Well, um, are you sick?"

"Cancer," Hilliard responds, nodding.

"Ah, man," Jude responds. "Sorry about that, Mr. Lafitte. Daddy didn't even tell me."

"I reckon it wasn't his place to spread my business," Hilliard says. "Anyway, I'll be fine. But I wish I could say the same about my pocketbook."

"What do you mean?" Jude asks him.

"The medical bills are kicking my rear end," he explains. "And that's why I'm going up on your rent almost double, son. I'm sorry."

Jude's mouth drops half-opened, shocked. He's drowning in debt and knows he won't be able to pay the increased rent.

But his response to Hilliard is, "But I've always paid on time."

"Yeah, and I appreciate it," Hilliard tells him. "It's only business; nothing personal."

"But Mr. Lafitte, I barely make enough money now at the plant," Jude explains. "How am I supposed to pay you increased rent now?"

"Not to be rude, son, but I don't see how that's my problem," Hilliard tells him. "I got enough to worry about."

"Man, I don't know if I'll be able to afford it," Jude says. "I mean, that's a lot."

"I know, but I've been giving you a sweet deal on the rent for six years now," Hilliard points out. "You won't find another property like this in Terrebonne

Parish for $500 per month.”

"I know,” Jude admits. "But I can't see how I'll be able to pay you a thousand bucks each month. I just don't. Are you raising the rent for that woman around the corner?”

"I am,” Hilliard says. "Not that it's any of your business.”

"Man, I was not expecting this news today,” Jude replies. "I mean, is there a way we can work something out?”

Before Hilliard can respond, Jude's cell phone rings from the empty chair near him. He grabs it and sees a Mississippi Gulf Coast area code. His face lights up, excited.

He looks at Hilliard and says, "Um, I got to take this!”

"Go ahead,” Hilliard tells him. "I'll wait out here.”

"Oh, alright,” Jude replies, walking to the door.

He then goes inside, leaving Hilliard on the porch.

***

Inside, Jude walks towards the sofa with the phone to his ear.

"Um, hello?” he says as he heads over to the couch and sits.

"Yes, may I speak to Jude Desonier?” a woman's voice asks.

"This is him,” Jude confirms.

"Hey, Jude, this is Derry with Hornsby Construction,” the woman says. "Did I catch you at a bad time?”

"No, ma'am,” Jude tells her. "I can talk.”

"Okay,” Derry says. "Well, I know you spoke to Mr. Hornsby a few weeks ago.”

"Right,” Jude affirms.

"Well, he wanted me to call and offer you the job," Derry continues. "It will only be for the summer, May through July, and the pay and benefits will be what he mentioned when y'all last talked. So, are you still interested?"

"Yes, ma'am!" Jude tells her excitedly, smiling. "Very interested!"

"Great!" she says. "Well, I will let Mr. Hornsby know. And I'll call you back next week to discuss the details."

"Yes, ma'am!" Jude responds. "And thanks for the opportunity!"

"You're welcome," Derry tells him. "And Mr. Desonier, we're looking for one more person to work on the casino this summer. Know anyone who would be interested?"

"A few folks from my old construction crew might be," Jude answers. "I'll touch base with them and let you know next week when you call."

"Sounds good," Derry responds. "Take care, Mr. Desonier."

"You too, ma'am," Jude tells her, dropping the phone onto the table.

He clasps his hands, places his palms at the rear of his head, and leans back on the couch, content. But suddenly, he sits up and sniffs the air as if something stinks. And he smells his armpits soon after.

"Whew!" he says, half-heartedly smiling.

He slowly leans back again. But, suddenly, his eyes widen.

"Crap!" he exclaims, leaping to his feet. "Mr. Lafitte!"

He races towards the door.

CHAPTER 3

Outside Jude's rental house, Hilliard is still sitting in a chair, tiny sweat bubbles forming on the top of his pale, bald head. Suddenly, the front door opens, and Jude walks out smiling.

"Well, your face and body language look way different from before you went inside," Hilliard says to him. "Good news, I take it."

"Yes, sir," Jude answers, smiling and sitting in a chair. "It's better than good. I got the job I've been wanting. It's only summer work, but it'll get me out of this financial crunch."

"Good," Hilliard says. "So, um, does that mean you'll be able to pay the new rent?"

"Yes, sir, I guess," Jude tells him.

"Well, where will the job be?" Hilliard asks.

"Mississippi," Jude answers.

"Mississippi?" Hilliard inquires, his brow furrowed. "Really?"

"Yes, sir," Jude replies, nodding. "In Gulfport."

"Ah, the Mississippi Gulf Coast," Hilliard says. "It's such a beautiful place."

"I've never been there, but I heard it's nice," Jude admits.

"Yeah, you'll love it there," Hilliard tells him. "Coastal Mississippi is beautiful. But Katrina probably didn't leave much to enjoy after it hit last year, much like it did here. In any case, what kind of work?"

"Construction," Jude tells him.

"Oh, okay," Hilliard replies. "Didn't you used to own a construction business?"

Before Jude can react, the front door opens. And Colt, a young man with a nearly perfect jawline and sporting a buzz cut, walks onto the porch. Jude and Hilliard turn around immediately.

"Aren't you Marcus LeDuff's son?" Hilliard asks Colt.

"Yes, sir, Mr. Lafitte," he answers, nodding. "Come on. You know that."

"Yeah, I do," Hilliard responds. "But I can't help but question how Marcus could raise such a... fine and ... upstanding boy. Anyway, um, since when did you start living here?"

"Um, I don't," Colt replies with a shrug. "Duh."

"Well, why on God's green earth did you walk out of this house as if you live here?" Hilliard inquires.

"That's what I'd also like to know," Jude interjects, looking at his best friend. "How did you get inside the house?"

"Duh, I came through the side window," Colt answers. "It's always open."

While Jude palms his face and shakes his head, Hilliard rolls his eyes.

However, Colt seems perplexed.

"What?" he says to Jude and Hilliard, shrugging.

"Oh, for God's sake," Hilliard mumbles, waving off Colt and standing. "You boys take care. And sorry about the rent, Jude."

He walks to his car, gets in, and drives off.

"What was that all about?" Colt asks Jude.

"He's hiking the rent," Jude explains.

"For real?" Colt inquires. "By how much?"

"Almost double," Jude tells him.

"Are you serious?" Colt says. "The nerve. If that old boy hadn't looked so pathetic, I would have whacked him upside his shiny bald head. What's the deal with him, anyway? He looked different. Is he sick or something?"

"Cancer," Jude answers, nodding.

"Oh, my bad," Colt replies. "I didn't know."

"Hey, it's not your fault," Jude tells him. "I feel bad for him. He said the medical bills are piling up. That's why he has to raise my rent."

"Hmm, I thought Mr. Lafitte was loaded," Colt says. "Didn't you?"

"How would I know that?" Jude asks, throwing his hands in the air. "I don't count other people's money."

"Well, I do," Colt responds, giggling. "And I ain't ashamed to admit it."

Jude grins and says, "Man, you are something else."

"I mean, I wouldn't be who I am if I didn't cut up now and then," Colt tells him.

Jude smirks and then becomes silent. Soon after, he sighs.

"So, what are you going to do?" Colt inquires.

"About what?" Jude asks.

"The rent," Colt tells him. "You won't be able to pay it based on what we make at the plant. But we can always get a place together and split the rent."

"You and me?" Jude asks. "Living together?"

"Yeah," Colt answers. "Why not?"

"Um, heck no, man," Jude responds, shaking his head.

"But, you're my brother... from another mother and my friend... to the end," Colt replies as he makes a sad puppy expression.

"Stop it," Jude tells him, trying to contain his laughter. "I wouldn't live with your filthy butt if you were the last person in Terrebonne Parish."

"Ah, so that's how it is?" Colt inquires.

"I'm just kidding, man," Jude tells him. "But I'll be fine."

Colt responds, "If you say so."

"I will," Jude says. "A few minutes ago, I received the call I had been waiting for."

"About the job?" Colt asks, his eyes widened.

"Yep," Jude answers, nodding and smiling. "They offered it to me. And they're looking for another worker. Want to come with me?"

"Heck yeah!" Colt answers enthusiastically.

Jude snickers and says, "I'm only kidding, man."

"But I ain't," Colt says. "I'm ready to get out of Terrebonne Parish and away from that old crusty plant."

"But it's only for the summer," Jude points out.

"I know," Colt responds. "But from what you told

me a few weeks ago, the pay and benefits will be great, and they will carry me through the end of the year."

"I mean, I was going to ask Timmy if he would be interested," Jude says.

"Timmy?" Colt asks. "You can't be serious. That old boy lives in Metairie now, driving trucks. Come on, Jude. I was the best you had on your construction crew. Let's team up again so we can make this money. What do you say, partner?"

"I mean, sure, if you're down," Jude answers.

"Heck yeah, I'm down," Colt tells him.

"Well, I reckon we need to look for a place to rent for the summer," Jude says.

"But it'll be difficult to find a rental there," Colt replies. "Katrina wiped out a lot of residential areas. Locals and contractors already occupy most of the rental properties."

"But we won't be able to make the daily commute," Jude tells him. "Neither of our vehicles is in good enough shape."

"Who said anything about commuting?" Colt says, smiling suspiciously.

"Well, what do you have in mind?" Jude asks him.

"My Aunt Eloise owns an old cottage in Biloxi, on the Back Bay," Colt explains.

"I didn't know you have kinfolks in Mississippi," Jude says.

"Don't we all?" Colt responds, smirking. "Anyway, Aunt Eloise doesn't live in the cottage, so it's just sitting empty."

"Think she'll let us stay there... for a reasonable price?" Jude inquires.

"Yeah, I don't see why not," Colt says. "I'm her favorite nephew."

"You're probably her only nephew," Jude says.

"Wait, how did you know that?" Colt asks with a shrug.

Jude shakes his head and rolls his eyes.

"But seriously, do you think you can make it happen?" he says to Colt.

"Heck yeah," Colt answers. "I got you. I'm your brother from another mother."

"Ah, right," Jude tells him. "And my friend... to the end. I got confidence in you, Colt. Now let's go call Aunt Elvira."

"It's Eloise," Colt replies.

The two men laugh and walk inside the house.

CHAPTER 4

A few weeks later, it's a beautiful, sunny day along the Mississippi Gulf Coast. Jude and Colt drive across Interstate 10 in Hancock County with the windows down, a cool breeze circulating inside Jude's faded-blue pickup truck. The lifelong friends rhythmically bob their heads to the sound of the upbeat country song blaring from the radio.

"Bro, this song is on fire!" Colt comments loudly from the passenger's seat.

"For sure!" Jude shouts as he drives.

"But it makes me wonder, though!" Colt yells.

"About what?" Jude asks.

Colt turns down the radio's volume and says, "If it's true."

"Huh?" Jude inquires, his face wrinkled. "You're wondering if what is true?"

"The song. Duh."

"Sorry, but I don't get what you're trying to say, man."

"I'm talking about the freaking lyrics, bro."

"Okay, but what about them?"

"Do you think the ladies really love country boys like us?"

"Oh, heck yeah," Jude answers with confidence. "Why ask such a silly question, man?"

"Just wondering," Colt tells him. "I mean, it's not like the ladies are lined up at either of our front doors. And we're both country boys."

Jude smirks and shakes his head.

"I'm serious, bro," Colt says to him. "It makes me wonder if we're ugly or something."

"What?" Jude asks, glancing over at Colt. "You need to stop tripping, man. You might look goofy, but not me."

"I reckon you're right," Colt responds, caressing Jude's arm. "Your exotic-looking skin is darned-near irresistible."

Jude yanks his arm from Colt, saying, "Boy, quit playing!"

"Oh, relax," Colt replies. "I was only kidding."

"Yeah, but you play too much sometimes," Jude says, chuckling.

"In all seriousness, though, you got a lot going on in the looks department," Colt says. "You have those gray eyes and that perfect five-o'clock shadow. I mean, what man you know has a five-o'clock shadow like yours? It's perfect. Then there's me. Folks only compliment me about my jawline."

"Colt, man, what are you talking about?" Jude asks. "You're starting to weird me out."

"You know me," Colt responds, laughing. "I'm just cutting up. But if your good looks aren't getting you anywhere with the ladies, there's no hope for me."

"There you go again," Jude says. "I'm not struggling with the ladies. Stop saying that."

"Well, when was the last time you went on a date?" Colt asks.

"Don't know," Jude answers. "Since I'm always working, I don't have time to go on dates."

"Yeah, right," Colt replies, smirking. "That's what they all say."

"I'm serious," Jude responds. "I work a lot, and you know it. But I do date."

"Well, who is the last girl you dated?" Colt probes.

"Okay, um, I think it was Aubrey," Jude says.

Colt laughs and says, "Y'all broke up six months ago."

"Yeah, well, it is what it is," Jude tells him, sighing.

"What happened to that relationship, anyway?" Colt asks.

"You know what happened," Jude responds. "She thought I was boring. Said I never liked to do anything or go anywhere."

"Right," Colt recalls. "I mean, why did she think that?"

Jude sighs and explains, "Because I never liked to go to the beach."

"That's right," Colt confirms. "I forgot you're allergic to the beach."

"I'm not allergic to the beach," Jude clarifies. "It's certain nutrients in the seawater."

"Right," Colt says. "It's still weird, though. You're the only person I know allergic to seawater."

"But there are others," Jude explains. "My momma is allergic to it. Anyway, man, I am tired."

Colt yawns and says, "Tell me about it. Why did you even come this long way? We should have come in on 90."

Jude glances at Colt and responds, "Are you being serious right now?"

"What?" Colt asks, shrugging.

"Come on, man," Jude exhorts. "Katrina tore the Bay St. Louis Bridge up last year, remember?"

"Yeah," Colt responds. "But I thought they were rebuilding it."

"They are," Jude confirms. "But they ain't finished. It should open back up next year."

"Whatever, Mr. Know It All," Colt responds, waving off Jude.

And Jude rolls his eyes and laughs.

"And back to Aubrey," Colt says to him. "Did you know she lives over in this area now?"

"Oh, really?" Jude asks. "Where?"

"Ocean Springs," Colt answers. "She works as a nurse at one of the hospitals on the Coast."

"How did you know?" Jude inquires.

But before Colt can respond, the faded-blue pickup truck splutters as if it wants to stop. And the men become concerned.

Colt sits up, looks at Jude, and says, "What's happening?"

"I don't know!" Jude answers, his eyes widening.

But when he glances at the fuel gauge, he discovers the problem. The vehicle is running out of gas. So he eases into the right-hand lane.

"What are you doing?" a panicked Colt asks. "What's happening?"

"We're running out of gas," Jude explains as he carefully pulls to the shoulder of the interstate and stops.

"You've got to be kidding me!" Colt shouts. "How in the heck did we run out of gas? Didn't you fill up before you picked me up?"

"No," Jude concedes, sighing.

"But when I first got in here, I saw the gas needle," Colt says. "It was at the full mark."

"I know," Jude tells him, turning on the hazard lights.

"Well, how did we run out so fast, bro?" Colt asks.

"Because I forgot the gauge doesn't work all the time," Jude confesses.

"And I thought I was the idiot," Colt says. "You need to get that fixed."

"Relax," Jude replies. "I'll get it fixed, but it was a mistake, okay?"

"I know," Colt acknowledges. "But what are we going to do?"

"I don't know," Jude says. "Can you call your Aunt Elvira?"

Colt smirks and remarks, "It's Eloise."

"Ah," Jude says, smiling. "My bad. I meant Aunt Eloise. Call her."

"And say what?" Colt asks.

"Just ask her if she can bring us some gas," Jude explains.

Colt sighs and says, "Okay then."

He pulls his cell phone from his front pocket and calls his Aunt Eloise.

CHAPTER 5

The bright sun radiates upon a quaint brown cottage surrounded by lush green vegetation, its overgrown grounds screaming for maintenance. A white, late-model minivan rests in the gravel driveway, from which a portion of the backyard lake is visible. And Aunt Eloise, a short, frumpy, gray-haired woman, slowly walks towards the house's green mailbox near the road. She makes it there a short time later and opens it. After pulling out the mail, she studies the parcels, oblivious to the faint sound of a ringing cell phone.

***

Inside Aunt Eloise's dated vehicle, the ringing cell phone noise is louder, the culprit likely being the small ringing phone exposed in an opened pink purse. And a Louisiana area code number flashes across its screen.

***

Back inside Jude's faded-blue pickup truck, Colt lowers his cell phone from his ear and sighs.

"She didn't answer," he tells Jude.

"You should have left her a message," Jude grumbles.

"But I couldn't," Colt responds. "It kept ringing."

"Darned," Jude says. "I'm all out of ideas, then. I don't know what we're going to do."

"I reckon we need to walk to a gas station or something," Colt suggests. "There's one back yonder off of exit 13. At least that's what the road sign said."

"Have you lost your mind?" Jude asks him. "We're on I-10. You know how dangerous it'll be for us to walk?"

"Well, we can't just sit here," Colt says. "It's also dangerous."

"Call Aunt Eloise again," Jude urges.

"And if she doesn't answer, then what?" Colt inquires.

"Just do it," Jude demands.

Colt sighs and calls Aunt Eloise again. But when she doesn't answer after several rings, he hangs up.

"Now what?" he asks Jude.

Jude shrugs instead of saying anything.

"I have an idea," Colt tells him.

"What?" Jude asks.

"Aubrey," Colt answers.

"All right," Jude says with a shrug. "What about her?"

"Call her," Colt suggests. "And ask her if she'll help us."

"Heck no, man," Jude responds. "I ain't calling her."

"Why not?" Colt asks. "She lives over here, and she might help us."

"Nah, I can't do it," Jude admits.

"Come on, man," Colt urges. "You know she'll help us. Do it for your brother from another mother and friend to the end."

Jude sighs and says, "Okay, I'll do it. But stop your whining."

But before he can grab his phone from the console, Colt's phone rings.

"It's Aunt Eloise!" Colt says, staring at the number flashing on the screen.

"Well, answer it!" Jude tells him. "Hurry!"

"Okay, okay," Colt responds, raising the phone to his ear. "Um, hi, Aunt Eloise!"

"Hey, Colton," she replies in a pleasant Southern accent. "I'm sorry I missed your calls. Everything okay?"

"Um, sort of," Colt answers. "But we need your help."

"What is it?" Aunt Eloise asks.

"Um, we ran out of gas on I-10," Colt explains as Jude looks on. "Think you can come to take us to a gas station?"

"Yeah, I suppose," she answers. "Strange that you boys ran out of gas. I don't understand that. But then again, I don't understand much you young folks do these days."

"Neither do I," Colt mumbles.

"What did you say?" Aunt Eloise asks.

"Oh, um, nothing," Colt lies.

"Oh, okay," Aunt Eloise says. "Anyway, what part of I-10 are y'all on?"

"Um, we're in Hancock County," Colt answers. "Not far from the exit that leads to Kiln and Picayune."

"Oh, I know where that is," Aunt Eloise says. "It'll take me a while, but I'll get there. You boys sit tight."

"Yes, ma'am," Colt responds, smiling. "And thanks a bunch, Aunt Eloise!"

***

Later, a dim bulb in the porch lantern and hordes of fireflies provide the only sources of light to the front exterior of the otherwise dark, quaint brown cottage. Aunt Eloise's white, late-model minivan remains in the gravel driveway, and Jude's faded-blue pickup truck rests by it. Besides occasional croaking from toads and hoots from an owl, quietness resounds outside.

***

Old, dark bulky furniture fills the interior of the cottage's dull living room, where Aunt Eloise rests comfortably in a recliner. And a sweaty Jude and Colt sit across from her on the matching sofa, two white ceramic plates containing fresh food remnants on the coffee table near them.

"Now that you boys are all settled in, I reckon I'll go," Aunt Eloise says as she stands. "It's getting late."

Colt glances at his watch and comments, "But it's only a few minutes after seven."

"Colton, I know what time it is," Aunt Eloise tells him, shaking her head. "I got to drive all the way to north Gulfport."

"Yeah, in that case, you need to go, considering how slow you drive," Colt responds.

While Aunt Eloise rolls her eyes, Jude looks shocked.

"Man, why did you say that?" he asks Colt.

"It took her forever to meet us in Hancock County," he explains.

Aunt Eloise shakes her head and waves Colt off. But then Colt laughs, stands up, and hugs her.

"I'm just kidding with you, Aunt Eloise," he says. "You know that, right?"

"Yeah, darling," she responds. "But I wish you would be more like your friend - Jude."

"You wouldn't be saying that if you knew the real Jude, though," Colt says, smiling.

"I'm sure he's a decent fella," Aunt Eloise responds, turning to Jude. "What did you say your last name is?"

"Um, Desonier, ma'am," Jude answers.

"And your folks are from Terrebonne Parish?" Aunt Eloise asks.

"Yes, ma'am," Jude answers with a nod.

"Hmm," Aunt Eloise says suspiciously.

And silence ensues as Jude and Colt stare at Aunt Eloise, who appears to be in deep thought.

But soon after, she says, "Anyway, I need to be going. You boys take care."

She then walks to the door and exits, leaving Jude and Colt.

CHAPTER 6

The following morning, sunlight streams through the partially opened drapes and onto the full-size bed where Jude soundly sleeps inside a dim, quiet room. Suddenly, Jude shifts and moves around. Soon after, he abruptly rises and glances at the brown clock on the nightstand. When he realizes the timepiece isn't on, he panics and grabs his cell phone. He stares at it.

"Oh, crap!" he shouts, realizing it is 7:25.

He leaps out of bed and flees the room.

***

Inside Colt's room, darkness reigns.

And Jude's voice suddenly resonates faintly, saying, "Colt!"

Suddenly, there's light from Jude opening the curtains. And inside the dim room, Colt abruptly lifts his head and stares at his best friend.

"What do you want, bro?" he asks.

"Get up, man!" Jude tells him. "It's almost eight o'clock!"

Colt's eyes widen, and he says, "What?"

He glances at the white clock on the nightstand next to his bed and sees it isn't working.

"What's going on?" he asks Jude.

"I think the power went out," Jude explains. "Get up! We got to go!"

"Dang, bro!" Colt responds, leaping to his feet. "We can't be late for our first day!"

"Tell me about it!" Jude says. "Hurry and get dressed!"

"What about breakfast?" Colt asks.

"What about it?" Jude says, shrugging.

"We have to eat," Colt answers.

Jude shakes his head and walks towards the door.

"We don't have time for that," he tells Colt.

"But I got to have breakfast," Colt protests. "Momma and Daddy always told me it's the most important meal of the day."

"Yeah, yeah, yeah, whatever," Jude tells him as he walks out the door. "Just hurry!"

***

On a beautiful, sunny morning, traffic is heavy along the Mississippi Gulf Coast. Jude's faded-blue pickup truck speeds down Beach Boulevard but constantly comes to screeching halts.

***

Inside the vehicle, Jude drives while Colt sits in the passenger's seat. Both men look distressed.

"I can't believe we're going to be late for our first day on the job," Colt tells Jude. "This is unbelievable!"

"Oh, relax, man," Jude responds. "We'll make it."

"Not the way you're driving," Colt says.

Jude glances at him and replies, "What do you mean by that?"

"Bro, you're driving like Aunt Eloise," Colt explains. "Go faster! We're supposed to meet that woman named Derry at eight!"

"Colt, chill!" Jude says.

"Don't tell me to chill, bro," Colt responds. "We could lose the job before we even start it. And quitting our jobs at the plant and moving over to Mississippi will be for nothing."

"Well, it won't be my fault if that happens," Jude says.

"Well, whose fault will it be?" Colt asks.

"Yours, for starters," Jude answers. "And your Aunt Elvira's."

"For the umpteenth time, it's Aunt Eloise," Colt shouts. "And how would it be our fault?"

"Whatever," Jude responds, waving him off.

"I'm serious," Colt says. "How will it be Aunt Eloise's fault if we get fired?"

"Because she should have told us she constantly has power outages in that old raggedy cottage of hers," Jude answers.

"I know you didn't," Colt says, his eyes widening.

"I didn't what?" Jude replies.

"Talk about Aunt Eloise's cottage," Colt tells him.

"Well, I did," Jude says. "That thing is raggedy!"

"Well, we're staying there for free!" Colt shouts. "And that cottage is a family heirloom!"

"With poor electrical," Jude adds.

"Well, you're an electrician," Colt says. "Why don't you fix it?"

"Well, maybe I will," Jude tells him.

"Good," Colt says. "That'll be nice of you."

"I know!" Jude shouts. "Because I'm a nice guy."

Awkward silence ensues as Jude drives, and Colt looks straight ahead. But a short time later, both men laugh out loud.

"Man, you are something else," Jude says, glancing at Colt.

Colt giggles and replies, "Well, I wouldn't be Colt if I didn't act a fool now and then."

Jude sighs, smiles, and says, "True. But if we get fired for being late, I blame you."

"Why?" Colt asks.

"Breakfast is the most important meal of the day," Jude states mockingly. "That's what Momma and Daddy used to tell me."

"Well, it is," Colt confirms.

"But we could have skipped it this morning," Jude tells him. "It'll be a shame if we get canned for being late because we stopped to get a sausage biscuit."

"It sure was good, though," Colt responds, laughing.

Jude smiles and says, "Yeah, you're right. It was good."

The men laugh again but abruptly cut it off when a police siren echoes behind them. They look in the rearview mirror to see a cop car with flashing lights.

"Crap," Jude grumbles, smacking the steering wheel. "Going too fast."

Colt sighs and says, "Yep."

"Just great," Jude replies as he eases to the shoulder of the road and turns into a lot designated for beachgoers, with the police car following suit.

And not long after Jude stops, he removes his wallet from his back pocket and takes out his driver's license. Soon after, he looks into the rearview mirror to see a hunched-back, gray-headed officer in sunglasses exit the cop car and approach the driver's side of his faded-blue pickup truck.

When Jude takes a deep breath and releases it, Colt tells him, "Just relax."

"Easy for you to say," Jude responds, just as the officer makes it to his window and motion for him to roll it down.

"It'll be fine, bro," Colt assures him.

But Jude waves him off and looks at the officer standing at his window.

He clears his throat, smiles, and says, "Um, hi, officer."

"License, please," the man responds in a southern drawl.

"Here you go, sir," Jude replies, handing him the license.

After studying the license for several seconds, the officer hands it back to Jude. He then takes off his dark shades.

"Where are you boys headed to in such a hurry this time of the morning?" he asks Colt and Jude.

"Work," Jude answers.

"What kind?" the man asks suspiciously.

"Construction," Colt answers from the passenger's side. "We'll be helping rebuild the Coastal Isle Casino."

"And who are you?" the officer asks Colt.

"Colt," he tells him. "My name is Colton, but I go by Colt."

"Uh-huh," the officer responds. "Anything else you'd like to add, son?"

"Um, no, sir," Colt answers as Jude shakes his head.

"Anyway, what part of Louisiana are y'all from?" the officer asks.

"Terrebonne Parish, sir," Jude answers.

The man smirks and says, "The swamps, huh?"

"Depends on who you ask, I guess," Jude responds.

"Yeah, it's the swamps," the officer replies, snickering. "Anyway, how long you fellas been in Mississippi?"

"Only a couple of days," Jude answers.

"You boys know anything about that bank robbery in Biloxi the other day?" the officer inquires. "Three people did it, and one got hit while exchanging shots with officers."

"Um, no, sir," Jude tells him. "We ain't heard anything about it."

"Uh-huh," the officer responds. "Anyway, did y'all bring anyone else with you from Louisiana?"

Colt and Jude exchange glances and then look at the officer.

"No, sir," Jude tells him. "It's just the two of us."

"Uh-huh," the man responds. "Which hotel are you boys staying at?"

"No hotel or motel," Jude tells him.

"We're staying at my Aunt Eloise's cottage on the Back Bay," Colt interjects.

"Uh-huh," the officer responds. "At any rate, I'm giving y'all a warning this time. But slow down."

"Yes, sir," Jude tells him. "I appreciate that."

"Un-huh," the man replies, nodding. "Anyway, you boys, have a nice day."

He walks away and gets inside his vehicle. After he drives away, Jude and Colt look at each other and laugh.

"Such a weirdo," Jude says.

"Yeah, that old boy didn't get cut from the right piece of cloth," Colt adds.

"You can say that again," Jude tells him. "Anyway, let's get out of here."

And the faded-blue pickup truck pulls out of the parking lot, onto Beach Boulevard, and heads west.

CHAPTER 7

Later, the Coastal Isle Casino site bustles with activity. Some construction workers congregate while others walk the grounds, occasionally going in and out of the gaming house that looks nearly complete. The sounds of chatter, laughter, table saws, hammering, and bulldozers echo throughout. Derry, an impatient-looking, petite, attractive young woman in stylish eyeglasses, stands near the entrance, continuously gazing at her watch.

Suddenly, Jude's faded-blue pickup truck speeds onto the property and pulls into an empty spot in the front parking lot. He and Colt exit the vehicle quickly and go to the truck's bed. But when they look inside it, nothing is there.

"Dang it!" Jude says. "We forgot our freaking tools!"

"Bro, this can't be happening," Colt adds. "What are we going to do?"

Jude sighs and remarks, "I reckon we'll have to use someone else's tools."

"That won't be a good look, bro," Colt tells him.

"You got any other suggestions?" Jude asks.

"Nah," Colt answers."

"That's what I figured," Jude responds. "Now, come on!"

The two men dash to the entrance, where Derry awaits. And her beauty immediately enamors Colt, who goggles at her. And she notices, blushes, and loosens up.

"Jude and Colton?" she asks the guys.

They nod.

Jude shakes her hand and says, "I'm Jude. Nice to meet you."

"It's nice to meet you also," Derry tells him.

Colt clears his throat and rubs his hands together.

Derry smiles at him and says, "And you are?"

"Anything and anyone you want me to be," he answers.

Jude nudges him in the side.

"Um, I meant I'm Colton," he tells Derry. "But you can call me Colt."

She shakes his hand, bats her eyes, and remarks, "Well, it's nice to meet you, Colt. Cool name."

"Um, thanks," he stammers as Jude looks on and rolls his eyes.

"Anyway," Jude interjects. "Um, to make a long story short, we forgot our tools. Do you think we'll be able to borrow some today?"

"No need," Derry answers.

"Ah, man," Colt says, palming his face. "Are we getting fired?"

"No," Derry replies, smiling. "It just means y'all don't need them today."

"We don't?" a skeptical Jude asks.

"Nope," Derry replies.

Both men breathe a sigh of relief.

"Well, why not?" Colt inquires.

"Because today you'll go through new-employee orientation," Derry explains. "Dad likes us to be creative when helping new hires learn about our company."

"Dad?" Jude asks, his forehead wrinkled.

"I meant Mr. Hornsby," Derry clarifies, smiling.

"So, Mr. Hornsby is your father?" Colt asks.

"That's right," she tells him, nodding. "I'm Derry Hornsby."

"Interesting," Jude mumbles.

"Anyway, I'll give y'all a complete overview of the company as we tour some of the buildings we've built along the Coast," Derry says. "It'll give y'all insight into the type of projects in our portfolio and the quality of work Dad expects."

"So, pretty much a tour?" Colt asks.

"Yeah, I guess," Derry answers.

"Well, I'm already familiar with the Coast," Colt replies.

"Really?" Derry asks.

"Yeah, my Aunt Eloise lives her," Jude explains.

"Ah, I see," Derry responds.

"Yeah," Colt continues, smiling flirtatiously. "I should be showing you around."

Derry blushes.

"Pay him no mind," Jude tells her.

"Anyway," she says, still smiling. "We'll visit some of the hotels, schools, and shopping complexes that Hornsby Construction has built. And we'll end the day with a surprise."

"Surprise?" Colt asks. "What kind of surprise?"

Derry giggles, saying, "You'll have to wait and see."

"I'm cool with that," Colt responds. "And to be clear, we still get paid for today?"

"Yes, of course," Derry answers, smiling and touching his shoulder. "Anyway, if you boys are ready, follow me."

And the trio walks toward a black convertible sports car.

"Dang, Derry!" Colt comments as they make it to the vehicle. "This is your ride?"

"Yep," she answers, smiling and getting into the driver's seat.

"Don't embarrass us," Jude whispers to Colt as he gets in the backseat and Colt in the front passenger's seat.

Soon after, the black convertible sports car speeds away from the construction site and turns onto Beach Boulevard.

***

After a morning of touring some of Hornsby Construction's completed buildings and in-progress projects, Derry's black convertible sports car pulls into the parking lot of a large, warehouse-type structure in north Biloxi.

"What is this place?" Colt asks Derry.

"It's the Maritime & Seafood Industry Museum's temporary location," Derry explains. "After Katrina destroyed their permanent location at Point Cadet, the City of Biloxi hired us to remodel this warehouse and transform it into a temporary museum. This is our company's first remodel."

"Really?" Jude asks.

"Yep," Derry answers. "Typically, we only do new construction. Anyway, I thought it would be a neat place to bring y'all. Not only does it showcase what we can do in the remodeling game, but it also sums up what coastal Mississippi used to be like. But when we go inside, stay clear of the retired locals who like to come here and share their tall tales with visitors."

"Got it," Jude confirms.

"So, is this place the surprise you mentioned?" Colt asks Derry.

"Nope," she replies, shaking her head. "But it'll be fun. Come on!"

The trio exits the vehicle, walks across the parking lot, and goes inside.

***

Chatter and laughter echo throughout the warehouse's interior, where tall petitions separate the Maritime & Seafood Industry Museum's different exhibits and galleries. The setup is identical to their old location. And people eagerly go in and out of each space.

But the Nydia, a large vintage sailboat hoisted in the atrium with its mast rigged, gets the most attention. The antique boat appears in impeccable condition.

"Wow!" Jude comments as he, Colt, and Derry go up to the ship. "This thing is huge!"

"You're not lying, bro," Colt adds. "This old boy is impressive!"

"You meant old girl," Derry corrects him.

But Colt looks perplexed.

"Huh?" he asks, scratching his head.

"You referred to the boat as a boy," Derry explains. "But the Nydia is actually a girl. In fact, most ships and boats are considered females."

"Okay, expert," Colt says jokingly. "How do you know so much about boats?"

"We have a boat, but I'm not an expert," Derry tells him. "But I know a lot about the Nydia."

"Well, tell us about it," Colt urges.

But Jude points to the placards surrounding the ship and says, "Those things contain all the information you need, Colt."

"It's okay," Derry interjects. "I don't mind. I used to be a teaching assistant at the museum's Sea and Sail Adventure Camp."

"Sea and Sail Adventure Camp," Colt says. "Sounds neat."

"Yeah, it does," Jude agrees. "What exactly is it?"

"It's a day camp in the summer for kids ages six through twelve," Derry explains. "Its purpose is to promote coastal Mississippi's original history and maritime heritage. There're many educational and fun activities and even field trips."

"Ah, I see," Jude replies.

"Yeah, I enjoyed being a teaching assistant," Derry continues. "And the kids were great. Last year was my last summer there. But anyway, y'all wanted to know about the Nydia, right?"

"Yep," Colt answers with a nod. "That's if you don't mind."

Derry smiles at him, blushes, and says, "I don't mind."

Jude smirks and playfully rolls his eyes.

"Well, um, let me get started," Derry says, her voice sounding professional. "The Nydia was built around 1898 at the Johnson Shipyard, located alongside Biloxi's Back Bay."

"Back Bay?" Colt inquires.

"Yep," Derry answers. "Why?"

"That's where we live," Colt responds. "I mean, it's my Aunt Eloise's house. But she's letting us stay there."

"Too much info, man," Jude interjects, shaking his head.

Derry laughs, saying, "Oh, leave Colt alone."

"Well, thank you, Derry," Colt comments.

"You're welcome, Colt," she tells him, smiling.

"Oh, my goodness," Jude says, palming his forehead.

"Anyway," Derry replies. "The Nydia is made of cypress and steam-bent oak. A university in Louisiana displayed it for a while before it came to the Maritime and Seafood Industry Museum."

"Ah, Louisiana," Jude remarks. "Our home state."

"That's right," Colt adds boastfully. "We're a couple of country boys from Louisiana, in case you didn't know."

"How could I forget with those accents?" Derry says, snickering.

"You're joking," Colt replies. "But folks consider us two of the most eligible bachelors in south Louisiana."

"Yeah, a couple of Terrebonne Parish's finest," Jude adds, laughing.

And Derry snickers.

"Anyway," she says a short time later. "Are you

guys ready to move on?"

"Sure," Jude answers.

"Where to next?" Colt adds.

"Um, let's go to the Wooden Boat Gallery," Derry replies.

"Lead the way, tour guide," Colt responds.

And the trio exits the makeshift atrium.

CHAPTER 8

Wooden boats of all sizes and colors fill the Maritime and Seafood Industry Museum's interim Wooden Boat Gallery as people stroll about, gawking at the vintage vessels from different eras. But Jude, Colt, and Derry focus on the informative placards near each boat.

"This is some interesting stuff," Colt remarks.

"Right," Jude agrees. "Where did the museum get these boats?"

"People donated most of them," Derry explains. "Some of these things are ancient."

"Yeah, I see that," Jude replies.

"They are still cool," Colt adds.

"Yep," Derry says. "Anyway, let's head to the Commercial Fishing Gallery."

And Jude and Colt follow her out of the interim Wooden Boat Gallery.

***

Vintage boating and fishing equipment fill the makeshift Commercial Fishing Gallery. After entering the room, Colt and Derry go to the exhibit containing mounted marine life and engage in thoughtful conversation. And Jude heads to the Charter Fishing Display, which includes a historical timeline of coastal Mississippi's charter fishing industry.

And not long after making it to the exhibit and staring at the framed black-and-white photos lining the walls, a short, thin, gray-haired woman saddles up next to Jude and looks at the pictures.

"My father worked the fishing boats for years before he passed," the woman says.

Confused, Jude glances around. But he quickly realizes the woman's comment had been directed at him.

"Um, ma'am?" he says to her.

"How rude of me for not introducing myself first," she replies, glancing at him. "I'm Donna."

"It's nice to meet you," Jude tells her as he shakes her hand. "I'm Jude. So, um, what were you saying about your father?"

"He worked the fishing boats several years before he passed," Donna replies.

"Oh, okay," Jude says. "Did he work here in Mississippi?"

"All over," the woman responds. "But mostly in Mississippi."

"I bet he had several exciting stories about being on the water, huh?" Jude says.

"Only one," the woman admits. "And it involved a mermaid."

Jude snickers and says, "Mermaid?"

The woman turns and looks at him with a grave expression.

"Yes, a mermaid," she tells him.

"Hey, I'm sorry," Jude replies. "I didn't mean to make light of your story."

"No worries," the woman says. "No one ever believes me. And they didn't believe Até either."

"Até?" Jude asks, his brow raised.

"It means father in Sioux," the woman explains.

"Ah, got it," Jude replies.

"A few days after Hurricane Camille in 1969, Até and his crew caught a mermaid in their trawl just south of here, near Ship Island," the woman continues.

"You're for real, huh?" Jude says to her.

The woman nods and adds, "According to Até, she was a beautiful creature with an orange tail. Although terrified, she mystified the men, and they didn't know what to do with her. So they left her on the boat to bring her back to the mainland. But during the voyage, her orange tail dried out and cracked open, revealing human-like legs and feet bound in a thick glue-like substance. She then jumped overboard and started swimming. And as Até and the other men stared at her, a beautiful orange tail gradually grew around her legs and feet. She then went underwater, never to be seen again."

"Um, wow," Jude responds, scratching his head. "That's one heck of a story."

"And it's true," the woman adds.

"Um, yeah, if you say so," Jude replies.

"It is," the woman tells him.

"Come on," Jude says. "We're talking about mermaids, mythical creatures."

"And like I already told you, they are real," the woman replies. "Before he died, Até claimed that several reside around an old sunken whale ship a hundred miles from the Pascagoula coast. And folks claim to have seen some in the waters near Long Beach, Pass Christian, and Bay St. Louis."

"Gosh!" Jude says. "You seem so serious right now. So I'll play along. Whatever happened to the tail the mermaid left on your father's boat?"

Before the woman can answer, Colt and Derry appear.

"What's going on over here?" Colt asks. "You two looked like y'all were having a deep conversation."

"I told him about the mermaid my father caught," the woman explains.

Derry and Colt laugh out loud, offending the woman and embarrassing Jude.

Soon after, Colt whispers to Jude, "Derry warned us about these old-timers and their tall tales."

As if she heard Colt's comment, the woman shakes her head and walks away.

"Now that she's gone, where to next?" Colt asks Derry, who still appears amused.

"The Biloxi Seafood Factory Gallery, I guess," she answers.

And the three of them exit the makeshift Commercial Fishing Gallery.

***

Aged machines and tools used to clean, process,

55

and package seafood fill the makeshift Biloxi Seafood Factory Gallery. As folks mosey about marveling at the antique equipment, Derry, Colt, and Jude skim the black-and-white framed photos lining the walls.

"Who are those people in those pictures?" Colt asks.

"They are mostly folks who worked in the seafood factories around here," Derry explains.

"So the seafood industry used to reign supreme here?" Jude inquires.

"That's an understatement," Derry tells him. "I'm sure it led to the creation of our annual Biloxi Seafood Festival."

"That sounds fun," Jude replies.

"It is," Colt says. "I went once with Aunt Eloise. So much freaking fun."

"Right," Derry continues. "Because of Katrina, we had to cancel it last year. But it's happening this year. There will be tons of delicious seafood, live music, and arts & crafts."

"Man, I might want to go to that," Jude says. "When is it?"

"It'll be in September on the Town Green," Derry explains.

"Darned," Jude says. "We'll be back in Louisiana by then."

"But y'all might find a reason to come back for it," Derry replies, smiling flirtatiously at Colt.

And Colt blushes.

"Whatever," Jude remarks. "Anyway, where to next?"

"Um, let's go to the Environmental Gallery," Derry answers.

And the trio leaves the makeshift Biloxi Seafood

Factory Gallery.

***

Several exhibits focusing on coastal Mississippi's environment, weather, and wetlands make up the interim Environmental Gallery. As museum-goers mosey about the individual displays, Colt, Jude, and Derry gaze at the exhibit focusing on Mississippi's Barrier Islands - Cat Island, Ship Island, Deer Island, Horn Island, Round Island, and Petit Bois Island.

"I didn't know Biloxi has so many islands nearby," Jude remarks.

"Well, technically, Round Island and Petit Bois Island are south of Pascagoula," Derry clarifies. "Anyway, all the islands offer great swimming and fishing and are unique in their own way."

"Okay, Ms. Historian," Colt says jokingly. "Keep talking, and tell us how they're unique."

Derry laughs and continues, "Well, all the islands are uninhabited. During World War II, the U.S. military trained dogs on Cat Island as a combat strategy. I heard Deer Island's name is based on its history of deer swimming there for safety during hunting season, but I'm not sure how true that is. Anyway. People like Horn Island because of its sand dunes and long stretches of beautiful beaches. Round Island has a lighthouse there from the early 1830s. It also acts as a coastal preserve for many animals. I don't know much about Petit Bois Island, except that it offers great swimming."

"But what about Ship Island?" Jude asks.

"Ah, the legendary Ship Island," Derry remarks. "How could I forget? It offers the most fun, but I won't go into detail."

"Why not?" Colt asks, shrugging.

"Because you got to see it for yourself," Derry answers, devilishly grinning. "And guess what?"

"What?" Colt says.

"That's the surprise that I promised," Derry answers. "We're going there when we leave here! And if we're done now, we can go."

"Alright!" Colt exclaims, high-fiving an equally excited Jude.

And the trio leaves the interim Environmental Gallery.

CHAPTER 9

Later, Ole Biloxi bustles with activity, and the nearby Small Craft Harbor operates in a similar ambiance. It's a weekday, but several folks stroll along its boardwalk with Jude, Colt, and Derry.

"It's a freaking Monday," Colt whispers to Jude and Derry. "Why are so many people here?"

"I guess taking advantage of the nice weather," Derry tells him. "Besides, it's the summer. School is out, and folks are vacationing."

"Good point," Jude says. "That also explains why the downtown area is so busy."

"Right," Derry confirms, stopping in front of a mid-sized royal blue yacht and bringing the trio's commute to a halt. "Another typical summer day in coastal Mississippi."

But Colt and Jude are confused about why they stopped.

"I get that," Jude says. "But, um, why are we stopping?"

"Guys, this is the Queenie Gal," Derry tells him and Colt, smiling and pointing at the blue boat. "And it'll be our ride to Ship Island."

"Wow!" Colt exclaims. "This is one fancy boat!"

"You ain't seen anything yet," Derry tells him. "Wait until you see the inside!"

"I can only imagine," Colt replies. "I can't wait!"

"Tell me about it," Jude says, goggling at the yacht. "I'm ready to get on it right now. So where's the skipper?"

Derry smiles, saying, "You're looking at her."

"You?" Colt asks. "Really?"

"Yep," Derry answers with a smile.

"I'm impressed," Jude replies.

"I know, bro," Colt interjects. "A beautiful, smart woman who can steer a boat! Very impressive!"

"Thanks, Colt," Derry responds, blushing.

"So, is this your yacht?" Jude asks Derry.

"Technically, it's my dad's," she explains. "But I can use it whenever it's available. Anyway, there's something you two got to do before we leave."

"What?" Jude asks.

"Change those clothes," Derry answers, pointing at the men's outfits. "There's some extra swimwear inside the cabin."

"Hey, what's wrong with what we got on?" Colt asks. "We got on some of the finest, holiest, and tightest blue jeans you've ever seen."

Derry smirks, saying, "Yeah, I see that. And they are not exactly what one typically wears on the island."

"Oh, Derry, you just broke my heart," Colt tells her jokingly. "I've had these jeans since high school."

When she laughs, Jude interjects, adding, "He's not lying. He used to wear those raggedy pants to baseball practice. I thought it was weird then, but I never questioned it."

"You guys are so silly," Derry replies, giggling. "Anyway, are you fellas ready to hit the open sea?"

"Heck yeah!" Colt answers excitedly.

"Well, all aboard!" Derry replies, smiling.

And Colt and Jude follow her onto the yacht.

***

Later, a shirtless Jude and Colt lie on the deck of the Queenie Gal as it skips across the vast, calm Gulf of Mexico. The lifelong friends bask in the sun as Derry steers the ship, occasionally bypassing leaping dolphins. And besides the faint humming sound coming from the yacht, a peaceful ambiance exists during the ride.

***

A little while later, beautiful Ship Island is bustling with activity. Chatter and laughter echo throughout as some people swim, fish, and snorkel in the emerald green waters while others play in the sand and sunbathe on the beach. And some folks satisfy their curiosities through hiking and shelling. But they all seem oblivious to the Queenie Gal that eases up to the dock and stops.

A short time later, Derry, Jude, and Colt exit the boat in swimwear. Before they can start walking toward the island, a tall, skinny, bare-chested, middle-aged man approaches them.

"Hey, Ms. Hornsby," he says to Derry in a

southern drawl.

"Hi, Fred," she replies with a smile.

"Want me to tie up the Queenie Gal?" he asks.

"If you don't mind," she answers, nodding and handing him the key.

"Not at all," he replies, nodding at Colt and Jude.

He then heads toward the Queenie Gal. And Derry, Colt, and Jude start walking on the boardwalk toward the island.

"Who was that old boy?" Colt asks Derry.

"Fred used to work for Hornsby Construction," she explains. "After he retired, he began working here part-time as the caretaker, mostly maintaining the place. He lives in a cabin on the south side of the island."

"Ah, I see," Colt replies.

"This place is awesome," Jude remarks, glancing around. "Look at all the people out here! I didn't expect this island to have so much."

"I knew y'all would love it," Derry tells him. "I mean, this place is amazing! It has drinking water, two covered picnic areas, clean restrooms, fresh-water showers, and a snack bar."

"But what is that?" Colt asks, pointing to a large, towering medieval-type brick structure.

"That's Fort Massachusetts," Derry answers.

"I bet you can tell me anything I want to know about, huh?" Jude asks

"It depends," Derry says. "What do you want to know?"

But Jude doesn't answer. Instead, he brings the trio to a halt as if captivated by the 1999 pop hit from an Australian duo, detailing a couple falling in love before even meeting, echoing in the distance. Soon after, he goes into a trance-like state as he stares at a beautiful, exotic-looking lady with dark hair, treading in the sea amid a circle of similar featured men and women. And as if she's in a daze, the mysterious beauty gazes upon him. But her actions are much to the dismay of the handsome, scowling lad next to her.

Noticing the weird encounter, Colt taps Jude's shoulder, freeing him from the trance-like state.

"Man, are you okay?" Colt asks him.

"Huh?" he responds. "Um, yeah, I'm fine."

"Bro, you might want to stop staring," Colt tells him as he nods at the angry-looking man in the water. "Old boy looks like he's ticked off."

"Yeah, but I'm not worried about him," Jude admits. "Do you see the lady next to him?"

"You mean the one that is looking at you?" Colt replies.

"Yeah," Jude answers, nodding. "She's the most beautiful woman I've ever seen."

"By the way she's staring, I think she feels the same about you," Derry says.

"But, obviously, she has a boyfriend, husband, or whatever," Colt interjects. "So, he needs to let it go."

"Who are you to tell me what I need to do?" Jude asks.

"Chill, bro," Colt replies. "What did you mean by that, anyway?"

"You've been fawning over the boss's daughter all day," Jude tells him. "And I ain't told you to let it go."

Surprised, Colt grabs Jude's arm.

"Dude, are you serious right now?" he whispers. "You really went there? I'm only trying to prevent that old boy from coming out of that water and knocking you out for staring at his woman. What in the heck is your problem, bro? That woman got you acting all tough and stuff."

After a moment of awkward silence, Jude sighs and shakes his head.

"Look, you're right," he tells Colt. "I'm sorry."

He then turns and walks away from Colt and Derry, heading towards the island.

"Jude!" Colt calls out as Derry looks on.

"I'm fine!" Jude replies, still walking. "Just need to clear my head!"

"But where are you going?" Colt continues.

"Don't know!" Jude answers, still trekking. "Probably to that fort over there! I'll catch up with you two later!"

CHAPTER 10

Later, Jude explores Fort Massachusetts as the sun goes down. Despite people occasionally passing through, he's virtually alone inside the ancient structure. And his isolation, coupled with his earlier blow-up with Colt, doesn't diminish his admiration of the centuries-old fortress.

"This place is remarkable," he says to himself, roaming the interior grounds of the D-shaped tower.

"Indeed, it is," a woman's voice says in a south Louisiana accent behind him, causing him to flinch and stop walking.

He turns around to find the gorgeous lady he had locked eyes with earlier. She's alone, and, up close, she's more beautiful to him than the first time he laid eyes upon her. But he keeps it cool, assuming her boyfriend or husband could show up any minute.

"This is, um, Fort Massachusetts," he tells her.

"Yeah, I know all about this place," she says, smiling.

"Oh, really?" Jude asks.

"Yep," she answers, nodding and smiling.

"Well, do tell," Jude replies. "I'm all ears."

And they start walking the grounds.

"Well, several years after the War of 1812, America started building Fort Massachusetts around 1859," the woman explains. "It was one of the last Third System forts built."

"Third System forts?" Jude asks. "What were those?"

"America built 42 of them along the east coast to defend against the British," the woman continues.

"Ah, I see," Jude comments. "What exactly did they use this fort for?"

"Well, it was used a good bit during the Civil War," the woman explains. "At one point, the Union army occupied it, which helped them capture New Orleans. In fact, several hundred Union soldiers are rumored to be buried on this island. The fort deteriorated over the years, but a historical agency restored it as best as it could in the 1960s. And today, tourists can visit the fort and the island throughout the year, except for the winter, of course."

"Spoken like a true tour guide," Jude replies. "Man, I am impressed. I didn't know all Mississippi girls were history buffs."

"Sorry, but I'm not a Mississippi girl," the woman says. "I'm a Louisiana native."

"Ah, I knew I detected a Louisiana accent," Jude admits. "Which part are you from?"

"Near Grand Isle," the woman answers. "After the

storm last year, some friends and I moved to coastal Mississippi."

"Do you miss Louisiana?" Jude asks.

"Yes, of course," the woman replies. "I returned from there a few days ago after my brother's burial."

"Oh, I'm so sorry to hear that," Jude tells her.

"Thanks," she responds. "But enough about me. I want to know about you. Um, where are you from?"

"Um, Louisiana, actually," Jude answers.

"Really?" the woman asks, surprised.

"Yep," Jude replies, nodding. "Terrebonne Parish. My buddy - Colt and I are living in Biloxi for the summer, though. We're construction workers helping rebuild the Coastal Isle Casino in Gulfport. Derry, the young lady you saw us with on the boardwalk earlier, is our boss' daughter. She's only showing us some cool places along the Coast."

"Oh," the woman responds, blushing. "I've seen her on the island before. I thought maybe she was your girlfriend or something."

"Nah, nothing like that," Jude confirms. "But I think Colt is sweet on her."

The woman giggles, which Jude finds attractive, and they both stop walking. They then face each other.

"Now that I know your friends' names, tell me yours," she says to him.

"Um, yeah, of course," Jude replies. "I'm Jude Desonier."

"It's nice to meet you," the woman says as she shakes his hand. "I'm Karina Arceneaux."

"It's a pleasure to meet you," Jude tells her, caressing her hand to her delight. "Um, hopefully, your boyfriend doesn't get upset when he finds out you met a new friend."

"But I don't have a boyfriend," Karina responds.

"Well, your husband," Jude adds.

"Not married either," Karina confirms. "I'm with no one."

"What about that guy next to you in the water?" Jude inquires. "He gave me the meanest look as if he wanted to tear my head off."

"Oh, that was Damien," Karina explains. "He was my older brother's best friend, and I'm like a sister to him. He can be very protective, especially now that my brother has passed."

"Oh, I see," Jude says. "Um, in that case, can I get your number?"

But before Karina can respond, a male voice behind them shouts, "Karina, what are you doing?"

The pair flinches, turns around, and finds a shirtless, scowling Damien standing. His stature and toned body rival Jude's.

And Karina appears somewhat intimidated by him.

"I got to go," she tells Jude in a panicky voice.

And as she runs toward Damien, Damien smirks at Jude as if he's won the first battle. And when Karina finally makes it to him, they turn and walk away. But not before crossing paths with Colt and Derry, who suddenly enter the fort's courtyard.

And as the two pairs bypass each other, Damien intentionally bumps his shoulder into Colt's shoulder.

"Hey, bro!" Colt yells, throwing his hands up. "Watch it!"

But Damien smirks, and he and Karina keep walking until they exit the fort.

And Colt and Derry make their way to Jude.

"Did something happen between you and old

boy?" Colt asks him.

"Not really," Jude answers. "But I think he was mad that Karina and I were talking."

"Is that the woman's name?" Derry asks.

"Yep," Jude answers with a smile and nod. "Karina Arceneaux. And Damien, that guy with her, isn't her husband or boyfriend."

"Ah," Colt says, patting Jude's back. "So you stand a chance after all."

"Whatever, man," Jude says, laughing and playfully pushing him away. "I just hope she doesn't turn out to be the one I let slip away."

"If it's meant to be, you'll see her again," Derry assures him.

"Yeah, I hope so," he tells her. "Anyway, let's finish exploring the rest of the island."

CHAPTER 11

Several days later, rain pours down from the dark sky, soaking the grounds of Two-Step Toots, a country bar on Highway 90 in Ocean Springs. Several vehicles, including Jude's faded-blue pickup truck and Derry's black convertible sports car, fill the saloon's side parking lot.

***

Inside the lively roadhouse, conversations, laughter, and country music echo abound. While some people show off their latest moves on the dance floor or drink at the elongated bar, others chow down on nachos, chicken wings, or burgers. Folks like Jude, Derry, and Colt opt for a more laid-back approach, sitting and chatting at a booth near the back, by the restrooms, oblivious to Damien staring at them from the opposite side of the bar.

"I'm so glad it's freaking Friday!" Colt says, picking up one of the beers.

"I'll drink to that, bud," Jude replies, grabbing a beer.

"Me too," Derry adds, picking up the last drink. And the trio toasts.

"Man, it's been a long week," Colt remarks as he sips his drink.

"You aren't lying about that, bro," Jude replies.

"Yeah, tell me about it," Derry adds.

"What are you whining about?" Colt asks her. "You didn't work in the blistering sun all week long."

Derry's eyes widen, and her mouth drops half-open. Soon after, she looks at Jude.

"I'm not in that," he tells her, smiling and shrugging.

Derry playfully hits Colt's arm, saying, "How dare you, Colton LeDuff! I might not work outside in the heat, but I'll have you know that I still work hard. I mean, it's not easy whipping you into shape and transforming you into the perfect boyfriend."

"I agree with the last part," Colt replies, sipping the beer. "And you have done a great job with me in such a short period."

Derry gives him a peck on the lips and says, "Thanks, babe."

"Oh, cut it out," Jude tells them. "Go get a freaking room, for Pete's sake."

"Don't be mad, bro," Colt replies. "We'll help you find your true love."

"Right," Derry adds. "I got several friends who would love to go out with you. So, um, what characteristics are you looking for?"

"None," Jude answers, sipping the beer. "I'm

fine."

"Bro, we're only trying to hook you up," Colt interjects.

"But I'm good," Jude explains. "You and Derry have been in a relationship for not even a week, and now y'all are trying to give me dating advice and fix me up with random girls. I promise you I'm doing okay. Plus, I already met someone, remember?"

"Who?" Colt asks, confused.

"Karina," Jude answers as Damien grimaces in the background as if he hears the conversation.

"The girl he met at Ship Island," Derry adds.

"Oh, her?" Colt says. "I think that's a lost cause."

"But I don't care what you think," Jude tells him sharply.

"And that's the right attitude," Derry admits. "As I told you back at the island, your paths will cross again if it's meant to be."

"I'll see her again," Jude says confidently, Damien scowling in the background and abruptly exiting the bar. "You can bank on that."

"Well, I think you and Derry have had too much to drink," Colt replies. "Because both of y'all are tripping."

"Whatever," Jude tells him, waving him off. "Look, enough about my love life."

"Right," Derry says, standing as an upbeat country song suddenly echoes from the jukebox in the corner. "Now it's time to dance!"

And the trio makes their way to the dance floor and joins others engaged in line dancing.

***

A little while later, the storm continues drenching Two-Step Toots. Damien slowly bypasses vehicle after vehicle in the side parking lot, unbothered by the heavy rain. When he comes across Jude's faded-blue pickup truck a short time later, he stops and devilishly smiles.

He then glances around to ensure the coast is clear. And when he feels confident, he removes a wooden knife from his pocket, leans down, and drives it deep within Jude's rear passenger's side tire.

"You'll never have her," he mumbles, standing up straight and staring down at the wooden blade stuck in the tire.

Suddenly, the bar's side door opens, and a group of rowdy patrons exit. But Damien smiles and casually starts walking away, whistling in the rain.

***

Back inside Two-Step Toots, Jude, Colt, and Derry are still line dancing and having a great time. Their moves rival those of the other dancers, some of whom are tipsy. But, everyone is behaving and having fun. And a short time later, the music ends, and all the dancers disperse to their respective pre-dance areas of the bar.

At their booth near the back by the restrooms, sweaty Jude, Colton, and Derry appear exhausted.

"That was so much fun," Derry says, wiping her forehead with a napkin.

"I know, right?" Colt adds. "I ain't danced that much in I don't know how long."

"For real, though, bro," Jude replies. "I am worn out, and my head is killing me."

"Got anything for pain?" Colt asks Derry.

"Sorry," she answers, shaking her head. "I normally keep some in my purse, but I didn't bring it with me tonight."

"Sorry, bro," Colt tells Jude.

"It's all good," he replies. "I'll stop by the store on the way home to get some. You ready?"

"Nah," Colt tells him. "I'm going to hang around for a little while longer. Derry will bring me home."

"Cool," Jude says as he stands. "Well, I'm going to get out of here. Y'all have fun."

"Will do," Colt replies. "And be careful. The rain is coming down pretty hard out there."

"Got it," Jude confirms, walking away and exiting the bar.

CHAPTER 12

Later, heavy rain continues pouring from the black sky, nearly flooding a portion of the road in front of East Beach Pharmacy in downtown Ocean Springs. A few vehicles, including Jude's faded-blue pickup truck, occupy the parking spots along the partially submerged street.

***

Besides elevator music faintly echoing from the speakers in the ceiling, quietness dominates inside. Only a couple of people are roaming the store and browsing the shelves. And even fewer folks, such as Jude, are standing in line at the register.

Waiting, he grabs a newspaper from the rack and stares at the front-page story detailing the Biloxi bank robbery. As he skims the article, a bolt of lightning flashes on the other side of the window behind the clerk, and five seconds later, thunder echoes throughout the store, shaking the building and causing Jude to flinch.

"Whoa!" he says, dropping the newspaper and hastily scooping it up again.

Embarrassed, he returns the newspaper back to the rack. And suddenly, his cell phone rings. He sifts through his front pocket, pulls out the phone, and glances at it. And when Colt's name flashes across the screen, he answers it quickly.

"Hey, man," he says. "What's going on?"

"Nothing much, bro," Colt responds. "We're on our way to the house. I figured I'd check on you. The weather is getting bad out here."

"Yeah, I can tell," Jude says. "How far are y'all from the house?"

"Probably about another fifteen minutes," Colt tells him. "Where are you?"

"In the line at the pharmacy in Ocean Springs," Jude answers.

"How long have you been in that place?" Colts asks. "I mean, did you go to Gautier and Moss Point too? Dude, you left the bar way before us."

"Yeah, but I had to stop and get some gas," Jude explains.

"Oh, okay," Colt tells him. "Well, be careful out there, bro. The entire coast is under a severe weather threat."

"For real?" Jude replies.

"Yep," Colt answers. "So you shouldn't speed in that old raggedy truck."

Jude laughs, saying, "Whatever, man. I'll just see you later on at the house."

When he stuffs the phone inside his pocket, the woman in front of him completes her purchase and leaves. Soon after, Jude steps to the counter and hands the bottle of aspirin to the clerk.

***

Later on, the rain, thunder, and lightning are more severe. And darkness dominates as Jude carefully makes his way up East Beach Drive, the windshield wipers moving quickly back and forth. And a slow country song reverberates from the radio.

And as Jude continues on at a steady pace, other drivers zoom by him, appearing in a rush. And suddenly, the beeping intro of a weather alert notice echoes from the stereo.

"This is not a test," the automated voice says. "Your area is under a tornado warning. Please take cover now."

"Crap!" Jude says, turning down the radio's volume.

And against his better judgment, he calls Colt. But when his friend doesn't answer after several rings, he hangs up the phone and throws it in the passenger's seat.

"I got to get home," he says, sighing and pushing down on the gas pedal.

***

Outside, Jude's faded-blue pickup truck goes faster and faster up East Beach Drive. And Damien's wooden knife remains stuck inside the rear passenger's side tire, which looks deflated.

***

Inside the vehicle, Jude pushes down on the gas pedal, moving at a high rate of speed. But suddenly, a loud popping noise echoes throughout.

Jude gasps, and his eyes widen.

"Oh, crap!" he shouts, losing control of the vehicle as it shakes, swerves, and bucks.

And the sound of a blown tire resounds loudly,

going, "Flap-flop, flap-flop, flap-flop."

Jude is terrified and bug-eyed. He breathes rapidly and grips the steering wheel. But the truck operates freely, and it suddenly slams into the concrete bollards along East Beach, crashes through them, goes into the sand, and hits the water hard, causing Jude's head to smack against the steering wheel. And he blacks out.

CHAPTER 13

Unadulterated darkness and quietness dominate.

Suddenly, a female voice softly says, "Try to relax, Jude. Calm down."

***

In a brightly lit, fully-functional hospital room, a young woman in pink scrubs stands over Jude, who's in a bed shifting around.

"Just relax!" the woman urges Jude, who has a purple bruise on his forehead. "You're okay."

A short time later, Jude blinks his eyes open and stares at the woman - his ex-girlfriend.

"Aubrey?" he says to her, confused.

"Yes," she answers with a nod and smile

"What are you doing here?" he asks her.

"I work here," she tells him.

"Wait a minute," Jude says, sitting up and glancing around.

And suddenly, he cries out after feeling severe pain in his legs and feet.

"Oh, my goodness!" he screams as he pulls the covers back, revealing scaly lesions on his legs and feet. "What in the heck is going on?"

"Try to relax, Jude," Aubrey tells him, pulling the covers back over his legs. "Your pain medication should kick in soon. You're in the hospital."

"Yeah, I can see that, Aubrey," he replies. "But why?"

"Um, you had an accident, and your truck crashed into the ocean," she explains. "A man found you lying in the sand unconscious and called 911. And a woman also called. Anyway, you've been in the hospital for a few hours."

But Jude is confused.

"Huh?" he says. "Accident? What are you talking about? I mean, where?"

"East Beach over in Ocean Springs," Aubrey tells him. "When we dated, you told me you were allergic to seawater. So I guessed that's why you have painful lesions on your legs and feet. Do you remember anything about the accident?"

"No," Jude answers, shaking his head.

"Think long and hard, Jude," Aubrey urges him. "Because there is a cop in the waiting room with your parents. And he wants to talk to you."

"To me?" Jude asks, biting his bottom lip. "Why?"

"You tell me," Aubrey responds. "I smell alcohol

on your breath."

"Are you insinuating I was drunk?" Jude says, grimacing and still in obvious pain. "Come on, Aubrey. You know me better than that."

"Look, I know you," Aubrey tells him. "And I believe you. But you might have to work harder to convince that cop. Anyway, um, are you ready to speak with him?"

"Yeah, I guess," Jude answers, gritting his teeth from the ongoing pain and discomfort. "I ain't got a thing to hide."

"Okay," Aubrey replies. "I'll go get him. And I'll let your parents know you're fine and awake. They'll be able to come in after the cop leaves."

"Thanks," Jude says to her as she leaves the room. He then sighs.

"What is going on?" he mumbles to himself, trying to recall details of the accident.

But suddenly, the door opens, and a tall, dark-haired officer with brown eyes enters and walks to Jude's bed.

"That's quite a bruise you got on your head," he says to Jude. "How are you?"

"Other than pain, I'm fine, I guess," Jude tells him.

"Well, I won't hold you long," the officer responds. "But I got a couple of questions."

Jude sighs, saying, "Look, I don't know how I ended up here, but I wasn't drunk."

"I know," the officer replies.

"You do?" Jude asked, surprised.

"Your blood-alcohol tests and toxicology reports are normal," the officer explains. "Your truck might be slightly damaged, but you ain't in trouble."

"Whew," Jude says. "So, um, what questions do

you have for me?"

The officer holds up a plastic bag with Damien's wooden knife inside.

"We found this stuck in your rear passenger's side tire," the officer tells him.

"What is that?" Jude asks, staring at the knife.

"It's some type of wooden knife," the officer explains. "It likely caused you to have a blowout and crash on the beach. Anyway, um, you got any enemies on the Coast, Mr. Desonier?"

"No, sir," Jude tells him, grimacing in pain. "Not that I know of. My friend - Colt and I just moved here a few days ago."

"Yeah, that's what your folks told me out there," the officer says.

"I mean, do I have any reason to be worried, sir?" Jude asks him.

"Probably not," the officer answers, handing Jude his business card. "It could have been a prank gone too far. Some of these kids goof off too much around here. Anyway, I can see that you're still in a lot of pain. I'll keep you posted if I discover anything, and you do the same. Take care, Mr. Desonier."

"You too, sir," Jude says to the officer as he leaves the room.

He then nibbles his lip, wondering who would have stuck the knife inside his tire.

But suddenly, the door opens, and his parents - Joachim and Isabelle Desonier, come in with terrified facial expressions and rush over to his bed. While Joachim is a handsome silver fox of a gentleman with a five-o'clock shadow rivaling Jude's facial hair, Isabelle is a gray-eyed, graceful-looking beauty.

***

Healthcare workers walk back and forth in the hospital's brightly-lit fifth-floor hallway. Outside Jude's room, Colt stands at the cracked door, peeping inside.

***

Back inside Jude's room, his parents stand at the foot of his bed.

"The water, Jude," Isabelle says in a Louisiana accent to her pitiful-looking son resting in the bed. "We've told you to stay away from it!"

"Huh?" he says, confused.

"You heard your mother," Joachim clarifies. "You know you need to be careful around seawater. You're allergic to it, remember?"

"Pops, it's not like I crashed in the ocean on purpose," Jude argues. "I'm sure the officer told y'all that someone stuck a knife in my tire, which likely caused the blowout."

"He did," Joachim confirms. "And we'll discuss that later."

"But you also recently traveled to a local island by boat, correct?" Isabelle interjects as Colt looks on.

But before Jude can answer, Joachim adds, "I mean, that's what Colt just told us out there."

"Colt - of course," Jude replies, palming his forehead, oblivious to the bruise. "Ouch!"

"What's the matter?" Isabelle inquires.

"Um, I don't know, Momma," Jude answers sarcastically. "Could it be this enormous bruise on my forehead or the scaly lesions on my legs and feet?"

Isabelle pulls back the covers, revealing the sores on Jude's lower extremities. And she gasps.

"I'll be fine," Jude says, pulling the sheet back over his legs and feet. "Aubrey said the pain medication will kick in soon."

"Aubrey?" Isabelle asks, confused.

"The nurse," Joachim clarifies.

"Oh, her," Isabelle comments, rolling her eyes. "Well, her pain medication won't relieve your discomfort."

She glances around and back at the cracked door to ensure the coast is clear and doesn't see Colt. Soon after, she removes a brown paper bag from her purse. And she pulls two large sheets of seaweed out of it.

"What's that?" Jude asks her.

"Dried seaweed," she explains, covering his lower extremities with the marine plant. "It'll ease your pain and discomfort."

Starting to feel relaxed, Jude leans back in the bed and sighs. And Colt still confusingly looks on from the cracked door.

***

Inside the hospital hallway, a puzzled Colt walks away from the door of Jude's room and runs into Derry a short time later.

"Are you okay?" she asks him.

"Yeah - just shaken up a bit," he answers.

"How is Jude?" she inquires.

"He'll be fine," Colt answers somberly, recalling all the times he made light of his best friend's health condition regarding seawater.

CHAPTER 14

It's a beautiful Saturday in coastal Mississippi and roughly a month removed from Jude's automobile accident at East Beach in Ocean Springs. Despite the picture-perfect conditions, he feels anxious as he sits inside his front-end damaged, faded-blue pickup truck in a parking lot outside a burger joint on the beach in Biloxi.

After a while, he sighs, grabs his phone from the console, and calls Colt, who answers immediately.

"Hey, man," Colt says. "What's up?"

"Nothing much," Jude tells him. "I'm surprised you picked up."

"What do you mean?"

"It's just that you've been acting weird lately? What's up with that?"

"Um, nothing, man."

"Oh, it's something. We've known each other forever, and I can tell when something is bothering you. So talk to me and tell me what's been up with you. Look, it's just you and me. Derry ain't around to distract you."

"Bro, leave her out of this."

"Ah, I see I struck a nerve. Is that the reason you've been acting strange lately? I tried to warn you that you were falling for her too quickly. Is there trouble in paradise or something?"

"No, bro, we're good."

"I don't believe that for one minute. If everything is fine between y'all, why did you get all up in your feelings?"

"Because I love her, and I don't like when you talk about her, bro," Colt admits. "Is that so hard to understand?"

"Nah, man," Jude answers. "My bad. I get it. So, um, what's up with you then? Why have you been acting weird around me?"

"I don't know, bro," Colt tells him. "I guess I've been feeling bad for the times I tried to make fun of you for not being able to go swimming at the beach. During the night of your accident, I overheard you and your folks talking."

"You sneaky son-of-a-gun," Jude tells him, giggling.

"I know," Colt says. "But I didn't mean to. When I came to your room, the door was cracked, and I peeped in and saw you and your parents talking. I also saw those scaly lesions on your legs and the pain you were in. Seeing you that way made me feel bad."

"Ah, so sweet," Jude remarks sarcastically.

"I'm serious, though," Colt tells him. "And then to find out that someone stuck a freaking wooden knife inside your tire really shook me up. You're my best friend, bro, and I don't want anything to happen to you."

"I know, man," Jude says, sighing. "But I'll be fine."

"Yeah, you will be, bro," Colt replies. "Anyway, um, why did you call? What's up? I thought you were on a date with Aubrey."

"I am," Jude admits. "I mean, she's sitting on the back dining patio waiting for me. And I'm still in my truck."

"But why?" Colt inquires.

"Because I don't know if I'm making the right decision by going on a date with her," Jude admits. "We've had several great phone conversations over the past few weeks. But I just don't know if she's the one."

"What are you talking about, bro?" Colt asks. "Aubrey is a great girl!"

"Yeah, well, she wasn't so great when she broke things off with me the first time," Jude responds.

"Bro, it's all about timing," Colt says. "Maybe it wasn't meant for y'all to continue dating back then."

"But now is the time?" a skeptical Jude asks.

"Maybe," Colt tells him. "It's only one date, bro. Just see where it goes."

"Yeah, but I don't want to have regrets," Jude admits.

"What do you mean?" Colt asks him.

He sighs and answers, "I don't want to jump back into a serious relationship with her and wonder if the right one got away."

"Dude, what are you talking about?" Colt asks. "Are you still stuck on that girl you met at Ship Island?"

"Her name is Karina," Jude tells him.

"Yeah, her," Colt confirms. "Please don't tell me you still have the hots for her. Let it go, Jude. You ain't ever going to see her again."

After an awkward pause, Jude sighs, saying, "Yeah, I guess you're right."

"Heck yeah, I'm right!" Colt tells him. "Trust me, bro. So, go in there and have a good time with Aubrey."

"Just for you, man," Jude replies, smiling.

***

The dining patio has the perfect waterfront view of the Gulf of Mexico and the beachgoers having fun in the sand and water. But Aubrey, the lone patron, wearing a yellow tank top and white shorts, seems more focused on the book she's reading at the back table. And she doesn't even notice Jude standing in front of her. But when he clears his throat, she looks up at him.

"Oh, hi, Jude," she says, standing up and hugging him tightly. "How long have you been standing there?"

"Not long," he tells her, smiling and sitting down. "Good book, huh?"

Aubrey sits down.

"Yep," she answers, turning the front of the book towards Jude. "It's called The Flying Church of Orleans Parish, and it just came out."

"What's it about?" Jude asks.

"Well, a year after Hurricane Katrina devastates parts of Louisiana and Mississippi, a New York writer travels south to report on the region's reconstruction efforts," Aubrey explains. "When the young journalist arrives in Orleans Parish, he hears reports of people flying at The Church of God's Grace and Deliverance."

"Ah," Jude interjects. "So, will he unravel the mysteries surrounding the church and its congregation?"

"And that's the golden question," Aubrey adds.

"Hmm, sounds interesting," Jude admits.

"It is," Aubrey tells him. "

"You might have to loan it to me after you finish," Jude replies, smiling.

"Yeah, right," Aubrey says. "The Jude Triton Desonier I know can't stand reading."

"I see you still know me," Jude comments.

"Yep," Aubrey agrees, looking him in the eye. "Probably better than anyone, other than your parents and Colt."

They turn away from each other, and awkward silence reigns. But Jude turns and stares at Aubrey. Soon after, he clears his throat, and she looks at him.

"So, what exactly are we doing, Aubrey?" he asks her.

But she acts confused.

"What do you mean?" she replies to him.

"Since my accident, we've had great conversations over the phone," he explains. "But what are we really doing?"

"I thought we were trying to start over… to see if there's something still between us," Aubrey tells him.

"Is this only because you felt sorry for me at the hospital?" Jude asks.

"No," Aubrey tells him, shaking her head. "It's because when I saw you in that hospital bed, I remembered how much I love you. And that's the honest truth. And I hope you believe me, Jude."

He sighs and replies, "I do. Look, I'm sorry for coming on so strong. But I don't have time for games, and I know you don't either."

"Well, we are on the same page," Aubrey tells him, smiling.

"Well, it's about time," Jude replies, snickering. "After all the years of knowing each other, we are finally on the same page."

"You need to quit playing," Aubrey says, laughing. "Anyway, are Colt and that Derry girl still getting serious?"

"Like you wouldn't believe," Jude answers, nodding. "But I'm happy for them. She's an awesome girl, and he needs someone like her."

"Yeah," Aubrey agrees. "And now that we're getting back together, you no longer have to play the role of their third wheel."

"What do you mean by getting back together?" a male voice suddenly echoes.

They both look over to see a tall man with the build of a professional basketball player standing there, wearing blue sweatpants and a white V-neck t-shirt.

"Henry, what are you doing here?" a shocked Aubrey asks. "Are you stalking me or something?"

"I was having lunch with Mom when I spotted you," Henry explains. "Why haven't you returned my calls?"

"Because it's over between us," she tells him as Jude looks on. "We went on what? Two dates?"

"Yeah," Henry answers. "And?"

"After our second date, I told you it would be better for us to only be friends," Aubrey adds. "But you kept making it weird, calling and texting."

"Look, man," Jude interjects, looking at Henry. "The lady said it's over. You should leave."

"Well, no one was talking to you," Henry tells him. "This is none of your business."

"Well, I'm making it my business," Jude replies, standing up and looking at Henry, who has three inches over him.

"Oh, you're a tough guy?" Henry says, stepping closer to Jude. "Who are you, anyway?"

"Jude," Jude answers.

Henry smirks, saying, "Wait, seriously? You're Jude?"

"Yeah," Jude answers. "And?"

Henry looks at Aubrey and says, "So you mean to tell me you're getting back with this guy after he cheated on you?"

And Aubrey appears humiliated and embarrassed.

"I didn't cheat on her," a confused Jude tells Henry. "What the heck are you talking about?"

"Ask her," Henry says, pointing at Aubrey. "Don't ask me."

"What is he talking about?" Jude asks Aubrey, eyeing her suspiciously. "You told people I cheated on you?"

But Aubrey doesn't respond. And Jude gets agitated.

"Answer me," he demands of Aubrey. "Why is this guy saying I cheated on you?"

Tears well up in Aubrey's eyes. She rocks back and forth and nibbles her bottom lip while looking in Jude's direction, but not directly at him.

But when the first tear falls down her cheek, she sighs and then looks Jude in the eye.

"You have to understand," she says to him. "I was in a terrible place after we broke up. And I might have said some things that weren't true, but I didn't mean any of them. I'm so sorry."

"Unbelievable," Jude replies, waving her off. "You two deserve each other. I'm out of here."

"Please don't go!" Aubrey cries out. "Jude!"

But he leaps over the patio's railing and into the sand. And he starts walking away with his head down, Aubrey occasionally calling out his name.

But as the emotions start to overcome him, he begins running through the sand. And soon after, he glances back at Aubrey and Henry arguing on the patio. And when he turns around, he runs into a woman in a purple bathing suit top, blue jean shorts, a beach sombrero, and sunglasses, knocking her onto the ground.

CHAPTER 15

Jude feels embarrassed that he accidentally knocked the woman down.

"I'm so sorry, ma'am," he apologizes, extending his hand to her. "Let me help you up."

After she grabs his hand, Jude pulls her up to her feet. And he's surprised to see that the woman is Karina. His eyes widen, and his mouth drops half-open.

"Karina?" he says, smiling. "Is it really you?"

And she appears equally shocked to see him.

"Jude?" she says, removing her sunglasses.

He nods.

"Oh, my gosh!" Karina says, hugging him tightly. "It's you!"

Jude smiles as he pulls back and stares at her. And as he looks into her eyes, the onset of a flashback begins.

***

Inside Jude's faded-blue pickup truck on the night of his accident, he pushes down on the gas pedal, moving quickly through the heavy rain. But suddenly, a loud popping noise echoes throughout.

Jude gasps, and his eyes widen.

"Oh, crap!" he shouts, losing control of the vehicle as it shakes, swerves, and bucks.

And the sound of a blown tire resounds loudly, going, "Flap-flop, flap-flop, flap-flop."

Jude is terrified and bug-eyed. He breathes rapidly and grips the steering wheel. But the truck operates freely, and it suddenly slams into the concrete bollards along East Beach, crashes through them, goes into the sand, and hits the water hard, causing Jude's head to smack against the steering wheel. And he blacks out.

***

Unadulterated darkness and quietness dominate. But suddenly, Jude slowly blinks his eye open to find a woman in a dark-colored swimsuit pulling him by his legs in the sand while on his back. But his blurry vision prevents him from seeing her face clearly.

"What are you doing?" he mumbles.

But the woman doesn't answer. She keeps pulling him instead.

And a short time later, Jude tilts his head to the side and attempts to look behind him. And in his peripheral, he clearly sees his faded-blue pickup truck partially submerged in the sea.

And when he turns to face the woman again, he vividly sees all of her features, recognizing her as Karina, the beautiful woman he had met on Ship Island. And when the two of them lock eyes, she drops his legs and runs.

"Wait," Jude mumbles to her. "Don't go."

But she keeps running, and suddenly, everything goes black.

***

Back in the present, a surprised Jude stares into Karina's eyes as they remain face-to-face on the beach.

"You were there," he tells her, his eyes widening. "And you saved my life. But how did you know I was even on the beach?"

"Right place at the right time, I guess," Karina explains.

"Why did you leave?" Jude asks.

"I don't know," Karina answers, holding her head down. "I called 911, but I guess I still panicked."

"But why?" he asks, pulling her chin up and lifting her head.

"I don't know," she replies. "It's a long story. But I'm glad you're okay."

"Yeah, so am I," Jude admits. "And I'm even happier that I ran into you again."

"Yeah, you literally did that," Karina adds, smiling.

"Tell me about it," Jude replies with a smile. "And again, I'm so sorry."

"It's okay, Jude," Karina assures him. "I'm fine."

"I know," he replies, still smiling. "Look, I can't believe we're here together. I thought I would never see you again."

"I thought that as well," Karina admits. "But when I pulled you out of your truck the night of your accident, I thought that was fate. And so I kept hoping and wishing our paths would cross again."

"And here we are today, Karina Arceneaux," Jude interjects. "Let's make the most of our time together. Back at Ship Island, I already told you a few things about me, so I want to know about you."

"Fair enough," Karina agrees. "So, what do you want to know?"

"Everything," Jude answers. "Um, what kind of work do you do?"

"I guess you can say I fish," Karina tells him. "It's the only job I've ever done."

"I bet you get tired of eating fish then, huh?"

"No, fish will always be my favorite meal."

"So, how do you like yours? Fried, baked, or broiled?"

"It doesn't matter much to me."

"Yeah, I'm the same. So, um, where on the Coast do you live?"

"Don't laugh or think I'm weird when I tell you."

"I won't. Scout's honor."

"Scout's honor?" Karina asks, puzzled. "What do you mean?"

"Oh, it's just an old saying," Jude tells her. "I was only letting you know that I won't laugh or think you're weird when you tell me where you live."

"Oh, I see," Karina says. "Well, since my friends and I came to Mississippi last year, we've mostly camped out on Ship Island. Sometimes, we sleep in tents. But if the weather is bad, the caretaker lets us stay in his cabin. It has electricity and everything else we need."

"For real?" Jude asks.

"Yep," Karina answers, nodding. "It's not that we can't afford a house here on the mainland because money isn't an issue. We just prefer to stay on the island. It's so peaceful out there."

"Yeah, it is," Jude agrees. "The short time I was out there, I fell in love with the place."

"Are you sure it wasn't me you fell in love with?" Karina asks, laughing. "I'm only kidding, of course."

And Jude laughs.

"But seriously, I can see how anyone can fall in love with Ship Island," Karina continues. "The place is amazing. And whenever I feel stressed or out of sorts, I love standing on the pier overlooking the sea. The sound of the waves calms me a lot."

"Yeah, I bet," Jude tells her. "So, um, what about Damien?"

"What about him?" Karina asks, confused.

"That day on the island, you told me he was your brother's best friend," Jude says.

"True," Karina replies.

"Are you sure y'all aren't in a relationship?" Jude asks.

"Yes, I'm sure," Karina answers. "I promise. Why do you think differently?"

"Well, it seems like he has romantic feelings for you," Jude explains. "That's all."

"Well, as I told you, there is nothing romantic about our relationship," Karina states. "Yeah, we're close, but he's like a brother to me, and I'm like a sister to him. Besides, Damien is in a serious relationship with Jasmine, a woman in my circle of friends. She has an apartment here on the mainland, and I sometimes stay with her. She also has a boat that she keeps at the Small Craft Harbor."

"Ah, I see," Jude says. "Well, now that you have convinced me that nothing romantic is happening between you and Damien, can you actually give me your phone number this time? Damien ruined our moment the last time."

"I will give it to you on one condition," Karina tells him, blushing and bringing the couple to a halt.

"Okay, what is it?" Jude asks eagerly.

"You have to promise me you'll actually use it and call," Karina replies, taking a step closer to Jude and looking into his gray eyes.

"Ah," Jude says, stepping closer to her. "I think I can work out something."

"Are you sure?" Karina asks, batting her eyes and moving closer to Jude.

"I'm pretty confident I can make it happen," he answers, stepping closer to her and staring down into her deep, beautiful eyes.

CHAPTER 16

It's a few weeks later. And several vehicles, including Jude's faded-blue pickup truck and Derry's black convertible sports car, fill the Two-Step Toots side parking lot. After a month-long whirlwind romance, Karina and Jude are head over heels with each other. And finally, she agrees to meet him, Colt, and Derry at the trio's favorite country bar in Ocean Springs on a muggy Friday night.

***

Conversations, laughter, and country music echo throughout the roadhouse. While some people show off their moves on the dance floor or drink at the elongated bar, others eat the house favorites - nachos, chicken wings, or burgers. And while waiting for Karina to arrive, Jude, Derry, and Colt are talking it up in their usual booth near the back, by the restrooms.

"Bro, where is Karina?" Colt asks Jude, glancing at his watch. "It's after ten already."

"She'll be here," Jude replies. "She's just running a little late. That's all."

"A little late?" Colt inquires. "More like thirty minutes late."

"Oh, relax, babe," Derry tells him, taking a sip of her drink. "It just means we get to spend more time together tonight."

"Right," Colt says, leaning over and giving her a peck on the lips.

"Do you two ever stop?" Jude inquires, smiling and waving off the pair.

"Summer love," Derry replies. "What can I say?"

"And speaking of your summer love, I like Karina," Colt tells Jude.

"Okay, and?" Jude replies.

"But am I the only one who finds her strange?" Colt asks genuinely.

"Man, what are you talking about?" Jude replies.

"Bro, she lives on freaking Ship Island," Colt continues. "At least that's what she told you."

"But her story checks out," Derry interjects.

"What do you mean?" Jude asks, confused. "Are you doing reconnaissance on my girlfriend now?"

"No, nothing like that," Derry confirms. "I ran into Fred the other day in D'Iberville, and we started talking. And Karina's name came up. He confirmed that she and her friends stay on the island sometimes."

"Oh, her name just happened to come up?" a skeptical Jude asks.

"Yeah, I'm serious," Derry answers.

"If you say so," Jude replies. "But who is Fred,

and how does he know so much about Karina?"

"He's the caretaker of Ship Island," Derry explains. "Remember, he was the guy that tied down the boat for me that day we went to the island."

"The tall, skinny dude?" Jude asks.

"Yep," Derry answers, nodding.

"Well, there you have it," Jude says to Colt. "Mystery solved."

Colt gulps his beer and says, "Not quite, bro."

"What now?" Jude asks him, shrugging.

But before he can answer, Derry says to him, "Babe, what are you talking about now?"

"I think she's hiding something," Colt answers.

"Man, have you lost your mind?" a frustrated Jude asks. "What are you talking about? I mean, what can Karina possibly be hiding?"

"Babe, hurry and get to the point before this conversation gets awkward," Derry urges Colt.

"Sorry, Derry, but it's already way past awkward," Jude interjects.

"Okay, okay, okay," Colt replies. "Just hear me out. What have most of your dates with her been like? Either dinner and a movie at Aunt Eloise's cottage, a late-night walk on the beach, or a picnic on Ship Island, right?"

"Yeah, and?" Jude replies as Derry nervously looks on. "What's your point?"

"My point is that there is something off about her," Colt explains. "And I've thought a lot about what I'm about to say."

"Whatever, man," Jude replies, waving him off. "Just say it."

"Well, I think she and her friends are the ones who robbed that bank in Biloxi right before we moved to the Coast," Colt explains. "Think about it. On the day that police officer stopped us when we were running late for work, he told us that one of the bank robbers got shot and that he likely didn't make it. Didn't Karina tell you that her brother died around the same time?"

"Yeah, but that could be a coincidence," Jude tells him.

"Perhaps," Colt agrees. "But what about the way she just left you on the beach that night of your accident?"

"Yeah, that was kind of strange," Jude admits. "But at least she helped me and called 911."

"Yeah, but I still think she's hiding something," Colt continues.

"Look, babe," Derry says to him. "If you want to know so badly, just ask her when she gets here."

And before he can respond, a familiar voice says, "Well, I'm here now. Ask away."

Jude, Colt, and Derry look up to find Karina there. Dressed in dark jeans and a black tank top, she looks gorgeous.

"Hey," Jude remarks to her.

"Hello, everyone," she says, waving and smiling.

Colt and Derry return the greeting.

"What's up, Karina?" Colt says.

"Oh, nothing," she tells him. "I'm sorry for being late."

"It's okay," Derry tells her. "Love the outfit, by the way."

"Thanks," Karina replies, smiling.

"Well, take a seat," Jude tells Karina.

"Oh, no," she declines. "I kept y'all waiting long enough. Let's dance."

"Okay, cool," Jude replies as he, Colt, and Derry stand up.

"But first, I want to know what Colt wants to ask me," Karina says.

"Huh?" Jude inquires, confused.

"When I walked up, Derry told him he should ask if he wants to know something so badly," Karina clarifies. "I assume they were talking about me."

"Oh, yeah, um, that," Colt interjects nervously. "When Jude mentioned you are a fisher, I told him I wanted to know if you are a rod and reel girl or a trawler."

"Neither," she answers. "Why use either when you have a mouth and hands?"

And after awkwardly staring at each other for a moment, the four friends burst out laughing.

"Ah, a fellow amateur comedian," Colt comments. "My kind of person."

"I told you she's great," Jude adds.

"Now, let's check out her moves," Derry says, interlocking arms with Karina.

And the four of them make their way to the dance floor and join others engaged in line dancing.

CHAPTER 17

A little while later, in Two-Step Toot's side parking lot, Roscoe and Boogie, two muscular dopey-looking men dressed in all black, are sitting in a vehicle listening to the barely-audible local news on the radio. Suddenly, the back passenger's side door opens, and Damien, dressed in shorts and a t-shirt, gets in, closing the door behind him.

"What took you so long?" Roscoe asks Damien from the driver's seat.

"Shut up!" Damien commands. "And turn it up."

Boogie turns up the volume.

And the news reporter's voice echoes from the radio, reporting, "The FBI held a press conference earlier today at the Biloxi Public Safety Complex. The agency announced that leads are pouring in regarding the recent bank robbery. And they expect to make arrests soon. We'll have more on this story tomorrow night."

Damien sighs, saying, "Turn it down."

And Boogie turns off the radio altogether.

"Look, they're inside," Damien says to the goons. "They are likely sitting at the back table near the restroom. You know what to do, but don't harm the women. Understand?"

"Yeah, but how will we recognize them?" Roscoe asks. "Do you have photos of them?"

Damien pulls a folded piece of paper out of his pocket and hands it to Roscoe, saying, "No, but I have this."

Roscoe unfolds the paper, revealing a drawing perfectly depicting Jude, Colt, Derry, and Karina. Soon after, he shows it to Boogie. And the two goons laugh.

"Is this some kind of joke?" Roscoe says, looking back at Damien.

"Yeah, I would hate to think you're wasting our time," Boogie interjects, turning and looking at Damien.

And Damien grabs the men by the hair and pushes their heads together. He then leans forward and whispers in their ears. But shortly after, he lets go of their hair and leans back.

Roscoe and Boogie slowly turn and look back at Damien. Trembling, both men appear terrified.

While the frightened goons continue staring at Damien, he pulls a thick white envelope from his pocket. And he tosses it to Roscoe, who catches it.

"No need to count it," Damien tells him. "It's all there. And you'll get the other half after you complete the job."

And Damien exits the vehicle and closes the door behind him. He smiles and casually starts walking away, whistling.

***

Back inside Two-Step Toots, Jude, Karina, Colt, and Derry are still line dancing and having a great time with everyone else. But, a short time later, the music ends, and everyone goes their own way. While some folks leave the bar, Jude, Karina, Colt, and Derry head to the back booth near the restroom and sit.

"Now, that was a lot of fun!" an excited Karina says.

"Tell me about it, girl," Derry agrees. "You got some moves!"

"Second that!" Jude adds. "Where do you learn to dance like that?"

But, suddenly, Roscoe and Boogie appear at the table, denying Karina a chance to answer.

"Can we help y'all?" Jude asks the goons.

"Yeah, move," Roscoe demands.

"Y'all are in our seats," Boogie adds.

"Sorry, but there ain't reserved seating, old boy," Colt replies. "If you snooze, you lose."

"How about we make y'all move?" Roscoe says to the quartet.

"Oh, yeah?" Jude replies, standing up. "I'd like to see you try it."

Roscoe pushes him hard, making him fall back into the chair. And Karina immediately leaps to her feet and shoves Roscoe to the ground with superhuman strength. And soon after, she does the same thing to Boogie, much to her friends' surprise. A short time later, she leans down and stares into the eyes of the suddenly-terrified men.

The thugs then get up and run out of the bar, the patrons laughing at them. And Jude and Karina sit back down in the booth with Colt and Derry.

"Girl, that was awesome!" Derry tells Karina.

"Yeah, you're strong," Colt adds, making a muscle. "You must have outrageous upper body strength considering how you pushed those old boys down. What kind of workouts do you do?"

"None, really," Karina says. "But I swim a lot."

"Hmm, maybe I need to add swimming to my workout routine," Colt replies.

"Man, you ain't worked out since high school," Jude tells him.

"Whatever," Colt responds. "At least that old boy didn't push me down."

Surprisingly, Jude smiles, saying, "Yeah, he got me good. And you didn't even help."

"Bro, I didn't have time to get up," Jude replies. "Before I could do anything, Karina handled both of them."

"She sure did," Derry adds. "Girl power!"

"But Colt and I could have easily taken those guys," Jude says.

"I know," Karina replies as she leans over and kisses his cheek.

"I can't wait for you to meet my parents," Jude tells her. "They're coming over on the Fourth. I can't wait for them to meet the woman I've fallen in love with."

"You love me?" Karina asks him as Colt and Derry curiously look on.

"Yes," he answers, nodding. "And with all of my heart. I know we've only dated for a short time. But I've never felt this type of connection with anyone else, Karina Arceneaux. Um, what about you? How do you feel?"

"The same," she answers. "And it's scary. I've never loved anyone how I love you, Jude Triton Desonier."

And they stare into each other's eyes.

"Well, kiss already!" Colt blurts out.

Jude and Karina slowly move in on each other and kiss passionately.

But a short time later, Derry says, "Oh, get a freaking room, for Pete's sake."

And the four of them burst into laughter.

CHAPTER 18

A few weeks later, a bright full moon beams down on Aunt Eloise's dark, quaint cottage on a warm Fourth of July night. In the usual manner, the street lantern along the road in front of the property flickers, periodically scaring away the moths, mayflies, and beetles that have gathered there. Cicadas' choruses resound across the vast, green fields surrounding the house, not outdone by crickets chirping, toads croaking, and owls hooting. A white, mid-sized luxury SUV is in the gravel driveway, and Jude's faded-blue pickup truck rests next to it.

***

Jude, Karina, and his parents are sitting at the table inside the dusky kitchen. Dinnerware for four, containing fresh food and drink remnants, rests in front of them. And everyone appears stuffed.

"This was a great meal," Joachim remarks. "I'm full."

"Thanks, Pops," Jude tells him, smiling. "But Karina cooked it."

"Thanks, young lady," Joachim says to Karina. "You didn't mention earlier that you were such a great chef."

"Oh, I'm not that good," she replies, smiling. "But thanks for the kind words."

"Momma, what did you think?" Jude says to Isabelle.

"Of what?" she asks.

"Dinner," Jude tells her. "Did you like it?"

"Yeah, it was fine," she answers. "Considering we also had fish for lunch earlier today, I would have rather had something else. Nevertheless, it was good."

"Thanks, Mrs. Desonier," Karina says, fiddling with Jude's truck keys lying by her plate.

But Isabelle doesn't respond. And Jude notices.

"Momma, did you hear Karina?" he asks her. "She thanked you."

"Oh, sorry," Isabelle says to Karina. "You're welcome, dear."

Karina smiles and nods.

"So, Karina and I are going to the fireworks show on the beach," Jude remarks to his parents. "Y'all up for it?"

"Oh, no," Isabelle answers. "We're worn out from y'all showing us around all day."

"Yeah, we plan to turn in early tonight," Joachim

adds.

"Come on, Pops," Jude urges. "It'll be fun."

"I know," Joachim admits. "But we're exhausted. Plus, we got to head up to Hattiesburg first thing in the morning before returning to Houma."

"I understand," Jude replies. "But, can I run something by you real quick?"

"Sure, son," Joachim answers. "What is it?"

"Let's talk in the living room," Jude says as he gets up. "It won't take long."

"Okay," Joachim replies, standing.

"You ladies play nice now," Jude tells Karina and Isabelle as he and his father exit the kitchen.

***

Inside the dim living room, the local news is on the television. But the volume is low. Suddenly, the door swings open, and Jude and Joachim enter. They both sit on the sofa in front of the TV.

Joachim looks over at Jude and says, "So, what do you want to talk about, son?"

But Jude shushes him.

"One sec, Pops," he says to his father, grabbing the remote from the table and turning up the television's volume.

And the news anchor's voice echoes from the screen, saying, "The FBI has made arrests in New Mexico regarding the Biloxi bank robbery. And all three suspects will be brought back to Mississippi in the coming days for their initial hearings."

"About time," Jude comments sunts as he turns down the volume on the TV.

"That much of a relief, huh?" Joachim says.

"If only you knew," Jude tells him.

"So, what's going on, son?" Joachim says. "What

do you want to talk about?"

Jude glances towards the kitchen door to ensure the coast is clear. He then looks at his father.

"Karina and I have only known each other for a short time," Jude tells him. "But I love her, man. And I love her a lot."

"I know," Joachim responds. "After spending the day with y'all, I see you two share a special bond. And I'm happy for you, son."

"Thanks, Pops," Jude says. "With that being said, I want to spend the rest of my life with Karina. And I'm going to propose to her tonight."

"Wow!" Joachim replies, standing up and staring at his son.

"So you don't think I'm rushing into his thing?" Jude asks as he gets up.

"Not at all," Joachim answers.

"Good," Jude says. "Whew!"

"Congratulations, son!" Joachim tells him as he hugs him.

"Thanks, Pops," Jude replies. "Your support means the world to me. So, do you think Momma will give me Nana's ring to propose? I know she has it on it her."

"Yeah, she always carries it with her in that purse," Joachim says. "And she promised to give it to you whenever you found that special one."

"Exactly," Jude adds.

"But, son, I'm not sure your mother is all in on Karina just yet," Joachim admits.

"So you noticed also, huh?" Jude asks.

"Almost immediately," Joachim answers. "But all is not lost. Take a seat so I can fill you in on how to get her on your side."

And the two men sit back down on the sofa.

***

Inside the kitchen, Karina and Isabelle remain sitting across from each other, and the two women appear to be in an intense standoff. And after a while, Karina starts trembling.

"I can't believe you just said all that stuff about me," she says to Isabelle, tears filling her eyes. "You don't know anything about me."

"Au contraire, my dear," Isabelle replies confidently, smirking. "I know all about you and your kind. I had you figured out the moment we met this morning. And quite honestly, you're not right for my son."

"But Jude and I are in love," Karina says, her voice breaking and tears falling down her face. "Does that matter to you at all, Mrs. Desonier?"

"No, it doesn't," Isabelle answers. "So you can save the tears, honey. There are others similar to you and compatible with you, but Jude isn't one of them. I'll never approve of y'all being together."

"Be that as it may," Karina replies. "Jude and I are in love, so we'll be together, regardless."

"Not if I can help it, dear," Isabelle tells her.

Suddenly, the kitchen door swings open, and Jude and Joachim walk in. The men pick up on the tension immediately.

"What's going on in here?" Jude asks Karina and Isabelle.

But they don't answer.

"What happened?" Joachim asks Isabelle.

But she doesn't say anything.

Jude goes to Karina and says, "What's wrong, babe? Why are you crying? Just tell me."

"Ask her," Karina answers, pointing to Isabelle, grabbing Jude's keys from the table, and standing up.

She then walks towards the door.

"Wait!" Jude calls out to her. "Where are you going?"

"Outside to sit in the truck," Karina tells him, to his dismay. "I have to clear my head. Just give me some time."

And after she exits the kitchen, Jude scowls at Isabelle.

"What did you do to her?" he asks her. "Tell me now!"

"Oh, lower your voice, son," Isabelle replies.

"No!" Jude tells her. "I live here, so I can talk as loud as I feel! Now tell me what happened between you and Karina!"

"Well, answer him," Joachim urges Isabelle.

She sighs and rolls her eyes.

Soon after, she says to Jude, "I told her she wasn't right for you."

"What?" an enraged Jude asks. "Why did you tell her that?"

"To protect you," Isabelle answers. "And to ensure that you have the life you truly deserve."

"What?" Jude asks. "This is crazy! Momma, I plan to propose to Karina on the beach later tonight. I was going to ask you for Nana's ring."

"Oh, no," Isabelle replies. "Karina will never wear my mother's ring, so you can forget about asking."

"Whatever," Jude says, waving off his mother. "I'm going outside."

"Not yet, son," Joachim tells him. "Give Karina some time to herself."

Jude sighs and says, "Yeah, I guess you're right."

"It'll also give you and your mother time to sort things out," Joachim adds.

Jude turns to Isabelle and says, "Just so you know, Karina is the best thing to ever happen to me. And I don't need you to protect me from her. What did you even mean by that?"

"It's hard to explain," Isabelle answers, standing up. "But just know I acted with your best interest in mind."

"What does that even mean?" a frustrated Jude yells. "Stop talking in riddles, Momma!"

"Don't raise your voice at me," Isabelle says.

"Right," Joachim adds. "Lower your voice, son. Enough is enough."

"Whatever!" Jude says, waving off his parents. "I'm out of here."

He races out of the kitchen. And after his parents exchange dubious glances, they follow suit.

CHAPTER 19

The bright moon still shines over Aunt Eloise's dark, quaint cottage. And the sounds of crickets, cicadas, toads, and owls continue to resonate throughout the property. Joachim and Isabelle's white, mid-sized luxury SUV remains in the gravel driveway. But Jude's faded-blue pickup truck isn't there.

Suddenly, the front door of the cottage opens. Jude runs outside, his parents nipping at his heels. But they all stop when they discover Jude's faded-blue pickup truck isn't there.

"She's gone!" Jude shouts, pulling his phone out of his pocket.

He calls Karina's phone, but she doesn't answer after several rings. So he hangs up.

"She didn't pick up," he tells his parents.

"Try calling her again," Joachim urges as Isabelle nervously looks on.

But when Jude calls her again, she still doesn't answer. So he hangs up.

"She still didn't pick up," he tells his father.

"Hmm," Joachim says as Isabelle nervously looks on. "Where do you think she went?"

"I don't know," Jude answers, shrugging.

"Think hard," Joachim tells Jude. "Where could she have gone?"

"I, I, I don't know," Jude stammers. "Maybe she went to Jasmine's house."

"Who is she?" Joachim asks.

"She's one of her friends who has an apartment here in Biloxi," Jude tells her.

"Do you know where she lives?" Joachim replies.

"No, sir," Jude says. "But I believe Derry does. That's, um, Colt's girlfriend."

"Well, call her to find out," Joachim urges.

"I don't have Derry's number," Jude replies. "But she and Colt are together now. I'll call him."

And he calls his best friend, who answers immediately.

"Hey, what's up, bro?" Colt says.

"Um, Karina took off in my truck," Jude says quickly. "I think she might have gone to Jasmine's apartment, but I ain't sure. Can you ask Derry if she knows where Jasmine lives?"

"Well, hello to you as well," Colt quips sarcastically.

"Look, man," a disgruntled Jude says as his

parents watch him. "I don't have time for games! Can you please ask Derry if she knows where Jasmine lives?"

"Okay, okay, okay, relax," Colt tells him. "We ran into Karina and Jasmine several minutes ago on the beach. Karina seemed pretty upset, and it looked like Jasmine was consoling her. Anyway, um, Karina gave me your keys and told me to give them to you. I can literally see your truck in the parking lot now."

"Where did they go?" Jude asks.

"Jasmine said she was taking Karina home," Colt answers.

"Home?" Jude inquires. "Ship Island?"

"Yeah, I guess," Colt answers. "What's the deal, bro?"

"I'll explain later," Jude tells him. "Can you put Derry on the phone right quick?"

"Yeah, hold on," Colt says.

Soon after, Derry says, "Hey, Jude."

"Hey, Derry," he replies. "Look, um, I need a favor. I hate to ruin your date with Colt, but can you use your father's boat to take me to Ship Island?"

"I would, but I can't drive a car right now, let alone a boat," Derry admits.

"What do you mean?" Jude asks.

"I'm a little buzzed, Jude," she tells him. "Colt is officially the designated driver tonight. Too bad he can't drive a boat."

"Darned!" Jude says. "I can't drive a boat either."

"But I can," Joachim interjects.

"Really?" Jude asks.

"Yep," Joachim answers. "And I'm sure I can get us to Ship Island."

Jude cracks a grin.

"Well, can my father drive the boat?" he asks Derry.

"Does he know how to operate one?" Derry replies.

"Yeah, he's experienced," Jude tells her.

"Well, yeah, as long as he's careful," Derry replies. "Colt and I are on Edgewater Beach now. Swing by and pick up the keys."

"Thanks, Derry!" Jude exclaims. "We'll see y'all soon!"

CHAPTER 20

Later, a full bright moon casts its reflection onto the Gulf of Mexico as the Queenie Gal skips across the calm, murky waters. And a short time later, the boat eases to Ship Island's dock and stops. And Jude, who holds a boombox, and his parents exit the yacht soon after, only to find a lifeless island with no people or other boats around.

"I'll tie up the boat and catch up with y'all later," Joachim tells Jude and Isabelle. "Go find her."

"But this place looks like a ghost town," Jude replies. "I don't think she's here, Pops."

"You never know until you look, son," Joachim explains. "And you won't have to do it alone. Your mother and I will help you."

"But it'll take us a long time to search this entire island," Jude replies.

"Not as long as you might think," Isabelle tells Jude, sighing and pointing behind him.

He spins around to find Karina, whose hair is wet, standing several feet away on the pier, gazing back at them.

He smiles and waves at her, calling out, "Karina!"

"Jude!" she shouts, displaying raw emotion.

"Karina, I love you!" Jude tells her. "And I want to spend the rest of my life with you!"

"Well, come and get me!" she replies, jumping for joy.

Jude presses the play button on the boombox. And the 1999 pop hit, detailing a couple falling in love before even meeting, begins blaring. And Jude increases the volume to the maximum level and places the radio down on the pier.

He looks over at Karina, shouting, "I'm coming to get you!"

And he starts running towards her, the ballad echoing all around.

"I'll meet you halfway!" Karina replies, racing towards him.

And when they meet up a short time later, they hug. And after the lovebirds engage in passionate kissing, they look each other in the eye and smile.

"Wow, your hair is really wet," Jude says to Karina as the song continues resounding. "Late-night swim?"

"Something like that," she answers, giggling. "So, um, did you really mean what you said? You want to spend the rest of your life with me?"

"Yes, I mean it," he tells her as his parents walk up.

"But are you sure?" Karina asks.

"More sure than I've ever been about anything," Jude answers, getting down on one knee.

"Jude, what are you doing?" Karina nervously says to him, periodically glancing at Joachim and a disapproving Isabelle.

"Um, Karina Arceneaux, we've not known each other for that long," he says. "But I love you with all my heart and want to spend the rest of my life with you. I don't have a ring for you yet. But will you marry me?"

Karina smiles, her eyes welling with tears of joy. But then she frowns and humbly looks over at Jude's parents.

Jude abruptly clears his throat, drawing Karina's attention.

"So, what's your answer?" he says to her. "Will you marry me?"

"Of course, I will!" she says, smiling.

A delighted Jude quickly gets up and hugs Karina tightly. While Joachim appears somewhat happy about the young couple's commitment, Isabelle seems bitter.

"No!" she shouts as everyone turns and stares at her. "Y'all are making a huge mistake! This will never work!"

"That's right!" a male voice suddenly shouts from behind. "Listen to the lady!"

Everyone turns around to find Damien standing a few feet behind them, clutching the stereo.

"Damien?" Karina says, her brow furrowed.

"It's come to this, huh?" he says, tossing the radio into the sea.

"Why did you do that?" Karina asks, walking

towards him.

"Because he's a jerk," Jude interjects as his parents gaze on anxiously.

"Keep talking and see what happens," Damian says, removing a wooden knife from his pocket.

"Whoa, drop that thing, son," Joachim urges him.

"This has nothing to do with y'all," Damien replies, pointing the knife at Joachim and Isabelle.

"Damien, stop it," Karina begs as she finally makes it to him. "You're scaring me."

"So, it was you?" Jude angrily says to Damien, staring at the wooden knife he's holding. "You're the one who stuck that knife in my tire and caused me to have a blowout!"

"Did you do that?" a concerned Karina asks Damien.

"He doesn't deserve you," he tells her. "I'm the only one who can love you how you need to be loved."

"But I don't have romantic feelings for you," she tells him. "I'm in love with Jude."

"I'll never let him have you," he replies, grabbing her, dropping the knife, and jumping into the sea.

"Karina!" Jude shouts as he and his parents run to the pier's edge.

But there's no sign of Damien or Karina. And with no regard for his inability to withstand seawater or the fact that he can't swim, Jude dives into the Gulf of Mexico.

"Jude, no!" Isabelle screams in agony.

But it's too late.

***

Beneath the waves, Jude flails his arms and legs as he sinks deeper and deeper within the dark emerald green ocean. But, amid the chaos, he notices Damien and Karina swimming away. And he's taken aback by the sight of the beautiful mermaid-like tails in place of their lower extremities. Damien sports a silver tail while Karina has a pink one.

Jude's eyes widen as he sinks further. When he eventually lands on the bottom a short time later, unbearable pain shoots through his legs and feet. He feels like his lungs are expanding, so he cries out. But he doesn't use his mouth. And he becomes confused about why he hasn't drowned and his ability to communicate without moving his mouth.

***

A few seconds later, on the pier, Isabelle tells Joachim, "I'm going in."

"Are you sure, sweetheart?" he asks her.

"Sure as I've ever been!" she tells him as she dives into the water effortlessly.

***

Back in the sea, Jude continues suffering. Scaly lesions appear on his lower extremities, beneath the hem of his shorts.

"What's happening to me?" he cries out telepathically.

But, suddenly, he hears a familiar female voice echo behind him, calmly saying, "Jude."

He turns to find Isabelle behind him.

"Momma?" he asks, astonished and grimacing from the pain.

"Yes," she answers without moving her mouth. "It's me."

"What's happening to me?" he asks, grimacing. "And how can we talk without moving our mouths?"

"We telepathically communicate while underneath

the sea," she explains.

"But telepathy isn't real," he says to her, still clearly in agony. "None of this makes sense, including seeing Damien and Karina with mermaid tails. Is this a dream?"

"No," Isabelle answers, shaking her head. "It's all real."

"It can't be," Jude replies.

"But it is," she tells him, pointing to her lower extremities where a lovely purple mermaid tail emerges in place of her legs and feet.

And before Jude can say anything, Isabelle points to his lower extremities. And when he looks down, he sees a beautiful royal blue mermaid-like tail in place of his legs and feet. His eyes enlarge, and his mouth drops open.

"You're half merman," his mother tells him. "And I'm a full-breed mermaid. Your father is pure human. And he and my blood relatives are the only ones who know our secret. I know you have several questions, and I'll explain everything later. We have to go get Karina first. Come on!"

After Isabelle takes Jude's hand, they swim quickly through the dark emerald green waters, bypassing sea creatures of all sizes. And when they catch up to Damien and Karina a short time later, Isabelle lets out a piercing screaming noise that stops Damien and Karina in mid-water. They turn around.

When they see Jude and Isabelle, they are surprised to find the mother and son with mermaid-like tails similar to theirs. And as Damien and Karina continue to observe the pair, Isabelle's eyes, including the iris, sclera, and pupils, turn completely black. And Damien suddenly becomes terrified, letting go of Karina's hand. Soon after, Isabelle lets out another shrill cry again. And Damien swims off.

After the trio watches Damien disappear into the sea's realm of darkness, Isabelle's eyes go back to looking normal. Soon after, Karina swims over to Jude.

"So, um, you're a merman," she says to him telepathically, smiling.

"Half merman, to be exact," he replies, laughing. "So, what gave it away? The tail?"

"Yep, it's the royal blue tail," Karina answers, nodding and smiling. "The tail always gives it away."

"Ah, got it," Jude says. "And, so, um, you're a mermaid."

"Um, yep," Karina confirms, smiling. "But technically, I'm a half mermaid."

She then turns to Isabelle.

"I see that you're a full-breed," she says.

"Right," Isabelle replies with a nod.

"How did you know?" Jude asks Karina.

"Only full-breed merpeople can black out their eyes," she explains. "The blackened eyes let half-breeds like me, Damien, and you know that it's nearly impossible for us to physically defeat a full-breed in a fight. I'm not saying it can't happen, but it hardly ever does. I mean, half-breeds are strong, but full-breeds have the strength of twenty men."

"Ah," Jude says. "So that's why Damien got scared and swam off."

"Right," Karina confirms.

"And that explains why you were able to handle those goons that night at Two-Step Toots," Jude says.

"Exactly," Karina tells him.

"So, why don't I have your strength?" Jude asks.

"Because you haven't lived an aquatic life," Isabelle interjects. "We draw our strength from the waters."

"So, why didn't you tell me about this merpeople stuff?" Jude asks her. "I mean, it's who I am."

"I know, son," Isabelle says. "I just wanted to protect you."

"You keep saying that, Momma," Jude replies as Karina looks on. "But what do you mean?"

"For as long as I can remember, researchers have flooded the Gulf of Mexico waters searching for Civil War-era sunken ships," Isabelle explains. "Their voyages put them in a position to discover our existence. And once the world knows about us, we're at risk of being hunted or studied in research labs. When you were only a baby, one of those research teams spotted my mother along the Alabama coast."

"Nana?" Jude asks.

"Yes," Isabelle answers. "They tried to catch her but accidentally took her life. Thankfully, my brother recovered her body and swam away with it before those men could find it. And after that, I decided to abandon the sea forever. I vowed to never let you live an aquatic life that could get you captured or killed."

"And so you and Pops lied and said that nutrients in seawater were harmful to me," Jude replies.

"Yes," Isabelle answers, nodding. "And I'm sorry. But it was the only way we could keep you out of the sea. It probably wasn't the best approach, but I hope you can understand why we did it."

"I get it," Jude says. "But all of this is so weird and unbelievable. It'll definitely take some getting used to."

Isabelle nods. She then smiles and looks at Karina.

"I said some harsh things to you earlier," she tells her. "And I'm sorry. I can see that y'all love each other, and I won't stand in the way. And I won't lie. I still have concerns for Jude's safety. But now that we're all aware of each other's true identities, we can work together to stay safe and remain discreet. What do you say?"

"I'm good with that," Karina replies as Jude smiles. "But I do have a question. How long have you known my true identity?"

"All along, honey," Isabelle says, smiling. "From the first time I saw you this morning."

"Ugh, I got to do a better job to conceal it," Karina replies. "Because I didn't detect your true identity at all."

"You'll get better with age, dear," Isabelle tells her. "Anyway, we must not keep Joachim waiting up there any longer. Plus, we have a wedding to start planning. Any idea on a date?"

Jude and Karina exchange glances and then look at Isabelle.

"Um, no, ma'am," Jude says to his mother.

"Just a little advice," she says to the couple. "In our culture, an old wives' tale promises that the waters will grant lifelong good luck to couples who marry on the summer solstice, the longest day of the year."

"Right!" an excited Karina confirms. "I heard about that! But summer solstice has come and gone for this year."

"Which means we got roughly a year to plan our wedding," Jude interjects.

"And we'll need every minute to make it perfect," Isabelle adds.

"Thank you," Karina tells her with a smile.

And the three of them start ascending through the dark emerald green water.

***

Roughly a year later, Ship Island plays host to Jude and Karina's wedding on a gorgeous, sunny summer solstice day. While their guests wear typical beach attire, the bride dons a pink wedding gown and Nana's ring, and the groom sports a royal blue tux. As the duo dance amid their family and friends on a faux dance floor on the beach, their favorite song, a 1999 pop hit detailing a couple falling in love before even meeting, echoes around them.

And Karina stares up into Jude's gray eyes, saying, "This is the best day of my life, and I can't wait to go on this journey with you. I love you so much."

"I love you, babe," he tells her, smiling. "And you becoming my wife today is the perfect way to cap off this Mississippi summer adventure we started a year ago."

***

Standing on top of Fort Massachusetts, a shirtless and angry Damien scowls as he looks down at the newlywed couple dancing.

"This isn't over," he mumbles. "You two will pay. Especially you, Jude Desonier."

And he devilishly smiles, oblivious to everyone else on Ship Island.

ABOUT THE AUTHOR

Dr. Jason A. Beverly is a Mississippi author and screenwriter who often incorporates the use of tradition, history, urban legends, folklore, and supernatural elements in his stories to provide intimate glimpses into the fictional lives of Southerners. He has a strong appreciation for small towns and tree-lined streets. Ernest J. Gaines is his literary influence.

After graduating from Hattiesburg High School, Jason continued his studies at the University of Southern Mississippi and received his Bachelor's, Master's, and Doctoral degrees from there. In his spare time, he enjoys spending time with his family, watching movies, and keeping up with the New Orleans Saints and Southern Miss sports. In addition to *A Mississippi Summer*, he is also the author of *More Christmas Clues*, *Christmas Clues*, *Releasing Magnolias along the Mystical Railway: A Collection of Mississippi Ghost Tales*, *The Flying Church of Orleans Parish*, and *Mississippi Revival Roads*.

www.ingramcontent.com/pod-product-compliance
Lightning Source LLC
Chambersburg PA
CBHW061317120726
48001CB00002B/547